# DARK MOON

BY

## FRANCIS JOHN BALDUCCI

THE LIBRARY OF CONGRESS
Control Number: 1-1463292041

Balducci, Francis John, 1964–
dark moon / Francis John Balducci

**ISBN 0692228225**
**ISBN-13 978-0-692-22822-7**

*This book is a work of fiction. Names, characters, places and incidents are products of the author's imagination or are used fictitiously. Any resemblance to actual events, locales or persons, living or dead, is entirely coincidental.*

Front and rear cover designs, images and elements by the author.

Printed in the United States of America.

# Dedication

To my father, Dominick Robert Balducci (1924-2006).

*We find ourselves faced by powers which are far stronger than we had hitherto assumed, and whose base of operation is at present unknown to us.*

Wernher von Braun, 1956

FRANCIS JOHN BALDUCCI

# Prologue

The immediate task here for the author is to bring the reader up to speed on some of the details of our near-future world. To start, the Earth leading up to 2108 has been wrought with challenges and struggles that no scholar or expert of the century could ever accurately predict, or fully remedy. Throughout much of the twenty-first century, natural resources have been significantly depleted—even with the greatest of global conservation efforts. Oceans were depleted of much of their delicate ecologies due to overharvesting, and the pollutants that they contained increased to catastrophic levels. Greenhouse gases increased as well and, as a result, dramatic changes occurred in global weather. Severe weather events are more frequent with greater intensity, especially in coastal areas. Most of the Arctic experiences ice-free summers while the Thwaites Glacier on the West Antarctic Ice Sheet has fully disintegrated forcing global sea levels to rise six feet.

Despite this and more, the human population remained unchecked and increased dramatically. Although nature occasionally served a serious reminder of our fragility, humanity persevered nonetheless. Medical advances extended human life expectancy by eight to ten years further exacerbating the problems associated with the population increase.

At its greatest number in the twenty-first century, the world population reached 12.1 billion. The mass majority are living on the Asian continent. The population of the United States arrived at 509 million. Europe reached 712 million—the only continent to experience a decrease, much due to a major decrease in the number of births while significant increases of women entered the workforce. The population growth has placed significant pressure on energy, water sources, public health, transportation infrastructure, and the general environment. As humanity outgrew the planet, the asteroid strikes of 2091 and 2093 may have delivered the only significant check on the increasing human footprint.

The population increase also created serious economic stressors throughout much of the world. Leading up to the asteroid strikes, our global economy was on the steady decline. In some industrialized nations, particularly in the US, the median household income continued to drop while the marginal taxation on the wealthy remained relatively low. The result, the economy became increasingly stagnant: the middle class experienced a steady decrease in their disposable income, consumer spending power decreased while corporations resorted to reduce payrolls. Employment steadily decreased for several decades; poverty was on the rise.

Governmental intervention was either ineffective or nonexistent. Relief was diminishing to a slow trickle. China experienced similar difficulties.

However, the European Union, or EU, gradually outperformed the US and China in economic gains, social prosperity, and institution building. Starting with the treaty of Lisbon in 2007, the EU ultimately consolidated its banking system, adopted a single market, focused on commerce and agriculture, and propelled itself into an industrial revolution. Outward growth allowed EU productivity to quadruple; economic performance increased to new heights. Although the EU continued for some time as an intergovernmental organization, as a result of its new economic strength, its competitive power increased. Its collective nominal gross domestic product continued to surpass both the US and China, and its citizens experienced sizable standard of living increases. The EU excelled in unified public policy decision making throughout much of the continent. This included fair labor laws and workers' rights, universal healthcare, and a proportional income tax system. Meanwhile, legal victories advanced civil liberties and social equality. Dialogue moved toward full federation.

On March 14, 2045, a new nation occupied the landscape with the ratification of the EU Constitution by the European Union Parliament. One day later, former British prime minister and then president of the European Council, Giles Millington, was elected by an overwhelming majority to serve as the first prime minister of the EU. In Mr. Millington's important new role, he would serve as the public face of the sizable, fledgling nation.

Meanwhile, China experienced a temporary banking collapse and a slight asset slump, which slowed the pace of its economic growth. And, the US decreased investment in education and infrastructure while it quietly ushered corporate bailouts through the rear door. The geopolitical climate between these two nations was becoming hostile. Increasing numbers of people from both nations desperately propelled themselves forward into an abject future. Corporate interests shaped much of public policy, and these interests overshadowed citizen influence.

Within his first week in office, Mr. Millington met with both the US president, James P. Richmond, and the president of China, Xiang Ming. Trade agreements were pending, and additional talks were being planned with the leadership from India and Brazil.

In the Middle East, meanwhile, civilian uprisings in various countries acted as a primary catalyst for revolution and regime change throughout much of the region. New leaders emerged from the rubble. Upon ascension, they adopted increasingly-progressive approaches to governing that focused on nation-building, fiscal health, and strengthening diplomatic ties. As a result of this new leadership, which embodied ever-growing social changes, theocracies and centuries-old dictatorships transformed into non-secular republics and democracies. Nations intensified investments in natural resources, manufacturing, infrastructure, community restoration, and education.

The United Nations of the mid-twenty-first century, with the help of dynamic leadership, recognized the changes in the geopolitical landscape and continued to play a crucial role in maintaining peace during the steady rise of democratic nations. Success in global governance was largely obtained through society building, regional support, global trade agreements, and the balancing of world powers. Conflicts for territories dissipated. Armed violence emerged mainly through regime change from poorly-governed societies. The UN obtained broader legitimacy and has been largely effective while intervening in state disputes. The Security Council conferred legitimacy on the use of force and, at times, effectively denied it.

The G-20 leaders assisted the UN in bringing about reforms. This included an updated membership configuration of the Security Council and its selection process and the empowerment of the secretary general. The G-20 averted global recession, stabilized financial markets, coordinated regulatory reforms while bringing about economic stimulus.

Human rights have become a serious focus of the UN and the G-20 while geopolitical economic power shifted to the East. The UN leveled sanctions against China resulting from civil rights violations, which the Chinese leadership continued to deny. Something resembling a new "Cold War" emerged on the horizon.

Energy production continues to depend on fossil fuels. However, use of wind, solar, kinetic, and nuclear power steadily increases.

Human nutrition increasingly derives from genetically-modified livestock, fish, and seeds. This occurs to address great stresses on food sources resulting from the dramatic increases in human population and, especially, to increase corporate profit.

Water sources in the US rebounded after decades of hydraulic fracturing. Drilling ceased after widespread water contamination was reported. Notwithstanding, Lake Mead at Hoover Dam dried to critical levels. The water crisis in the southwest affected 25 million Americans. However, through increased harvesting and desalination, water resource management eventually led to a delicately sustainable useable freshwater system.

Transportation in highly-congested cities mainly consists of mass public commuting. In outer areas and major highways, automated self-driving cars, or autocars, are used widespread. Some use autoplanes to travel between states and counties. The commercial airways continue to transport people in the same fashion as in the late-twentieth century, while suborbital transportation was introduced in the mid-twenty-first century for transportation between vast oceans and continents.

In health and medicine, increased stem-cell research results in breakthrough cures for Alzheimer's disease, Parkinson's disease, diabetes, spinal cord injury, heart disease, stroke, arthritis, most forms of cancer, burns, and more. In 2041, research began focusing on *in vitro* genetic purification in an attempt to prevent most genetic diseases.

Regarding crime, justice, and punishment, the death penalty was abolished in the US in 2029 in favor of life imprisonment as the alternative. As a direct result of the significant increases in life sentences, the private prison industry experiences dramatic fiscal gains via boosts in federal and state contracting and a surge in profits from prisoner labor. At the same time, economic-based crime continues to increase when competition for legitimate employment tightens.

By the end of the twenty-first century, percentages in major religious denominations gradually shift: Non-religious, 52.1%; Christians, 16.7%; Muslims, 13.1%; Hindus, 6%; Buddhists, 5.7%; others, 6.4%.

* * *

What occupied some of the world's attention during the mid-twenty-first century was the steady interest in space exploration by private industry. By appearance, this happened as a result of increased pursuits in science and discovery. However, in reality, it occurred purely for profit.

Two years after Europe became a federation, the Outer Space Treaty of Monaco was signed in 2047 by the US, Russia, the EU, and Brazil, and it entered into force the following year. The treaty struck down many of the principles of the Outer Space Treaty of 1967 and the 1979 Agreement Governing the Activities of States on the Moon effectively allowing for the commercial exploration of the Moon and the relinquishment of responsibilities to private industry. It also reaffirmed provisions of the Commercial Space Launch Act of 1984, which allows the space frontier to be opened to the private sector. Although outer space has been regarded as the common heritage of mankind, power is on the side of privatization—or, at the very least, states lacked power to stop the private space industry. Mr.

Millington playfully referred to the Monaco treaty as a "mere scrap of paper." However, he believed that this diplomatic step benefited the joining nations and, quite possibly, the scientific community.

China was not a signer of this treaty due to global pressure to exclude them, and due to the fact that the Chinese leadership at the time showed no interest in signing—opting instead to explore space on its own. The China National Space Administration continued to maintain its Project 921 space station launched in 2022, and regularly launched taikonaunts into Earth's orbit mainly to repair satellites.

Mars manned exploration became a serious focus of the National Aeronautics and Space Administration, NASA, despite funding shortages. Even with several successful unmanned missions, which included the discovery of ice under the planet's surface by the rover Curiosity in 2013 and by the rover Verrazano in 2028, public policymakers regarded manned missions as ambitious but too costly. Sending astronauts would cost fifty times more money than sending robots. NASA's Dexterous Robotics Lab resorted to developing the Valkyrie Series 9 robots for continued Mars exploration.

On July 11, 2033, the rover Excelsior successfully touched down on the Mars surface and deployed Series 9 robot Harrison. After approximately two months of excavating near the Hellas Planitia basin, Harrison uncovered a very primitive form of Martian life embedded within the rock. It appeared insect-like, the size of an average housecat, and it was estimated to have inhabited the region approximately two billion years ago. The find helped bring about renewed interest in Mars exploration and helped usher in a new science named "marsology." NASA launched a few additional robotic missions to Mars before deciding on a manned mission. No other specimen was found in these missions, and the robots lacked the necessary intuition needed for further discoveries and sophisticated experimentation.

On August 8, 2037, two NASA astronauts landed on Mars, Richard Wheelock, a geologist, and Lawrence Musgrave, a biochemist. Together, they established Mars base Proteus at Hellas Planitia and immediately began work.

Two months into their research, and while on the verge of additional discoveries, deadly solar flares emitted from the Sun reached the Mars surface. Despite rigorous testing of the space suits prior to the mission, the flares were so severe that the suits failed and the ionizing radiation quickly killed both astronauts. Six months later, a probe carrying Series 9 robot Marvin landed on Proteus to learn more about the fate of these men. Marvin then attempted to complete the mission of Wheelock and Musgrave, but never uncovered any new specimens. For its final act before shutdown, Marvin laid a plaque on the Mars surface near the base. Inscribed on it were the names of the astronauts, a graphic of planet Earth, and the words, "Proteus Abandoned in Place."

* * *

Emmett Terrell started off as an aerospace engineer in Chicago, Illinois, before becoming, according to *Forbes* magazine in a 2044 exposé, one of the world's most powerful and wealthiest men. He served as the top civilian advisor during the drafting of the Monaco treaty for good reason—he had access. It was his plan to take the privatization of space exploration to a whole new level and beyond.

With the Mars manned mission setbacks and the overspending on the development of large, new manned space systems, NASA found itself grossly mismanaged and in a fiscal crisis. Other space agencies around the world were not faring as well.

Terrell realized that the time was right to launch his ultimate corporate brainchild. Shortly after the signing of Monaco treaty, he held several meetings with his longtime associate, Dr. Calvin Westbrook, a brilliant and sort-after astrophysicist and engineer. Dr. Westbrook's vision began early when he served as an intern with Moon Express Incorporated in 2011. Together, along with a panel of wealthy, international entrepreneurs, Terrell and Dr. Westbrook formed the Allied Space Exploration and Research Administration, or ASERA, in 2049. Terrell was named its chairman.

Newly-formed ASERA quickly obtained various top scientists and engineers from NASA, the European Space Agency, the Russian Federal Space Agency, the Canadian Space Agency, and the Brazilian Space Agency. Terrell emphasized, with the assurance of Dr. Westbrook, that there was wealth to be obtained in our own "backyard"—the Moon—and that all who joined ASERA would become shareholders.

It did not take long before NASA was entirely defunded and for ASERA to absorb its intrinsic value. The European Space Agency, the French National Centre of Space Research, the Russian Federal Space Agency, the Canadian Space Agency, and the Brazilian Space Agency shortly followed thereafter. The Guiana Space Centre was also among the first to be acquired by ASERA. The remaining scientists and engineers in these agencies transitioned over into ASERA. Aerospace corporations were lining up behind ASERA in preparation for submitting bids.

Meanwhile, the International Space Station, the ISS, which depended considerably upon international collaboration, lost funding after some nations no longer wished to contribute. Access to the ISS became entirely privatized after defunding of the European Space Agency, the French National Centre of Space Research, and the Russian Federal Space Agency. Many astrophysicists and particle physicists regarded it as an "orbital turkey" where no important scientific gains were ever truly made. Some tourism did exist for the station, but the industry was not gaining enough revenue to sustain itself. ASERA easily purchased the ISS for their future use. Also, after both the Soyuz and Progress spacecraft were defunded, ASERA promptly obtained them and dismantled them for scrap.

Historically, governments lead the way in space exploration while private industry followed in lockstep. However, while a new generation of space explorers and dreamers in the mid-twenty-first century ushered in a new culture of innovation and entrepreneurialism, elected officials from various governments abandoned national pursuits of space exploration mainly because of—as Russian President

Nikolay Mironov put it—"the unjustifiable high costs" associated with it. China is the only nation that continues to participate.

ASERA is headquartered within a complex of buildings in Chicago's Lakeview section. The Exploration Corps occupies the main building while Research and Analysis occupies a smaller building across a lush plaza. Research and Development is headquartered in Moscow, Russia.

The Exploration Corps is organized into a uniformed, paramilitary-style structure headed by an admiral that had yet to be named. Other ranks somewhat follow the naval model consisting of captains, commanders, lieutenant commanders, ensigns, and warrant officers.

After ASERA obtained the Guiana Space Centre as a launch base and transitioned it for their use, it acquired or constructed several other Earth bases—most of them previously served as bases for former space agencies. There are now two vehicle assembly and launch bases, one located at the Baikonur Cosmodrome in Kazakh Steppe, Russia, and one at Cape Canaveral, Florida. After ASERA acquired the facilities at Alcantara Launch Center, it dismantled it and constructed a vehicle assembly and launch base in Touros, Brazil. A research and testing base was established in Cape Spear, Canada, while a massive research and testing, vehicle assembly, and launch base was installed in Cape Wrath, United Kingdom. Each Earth base houses individual Exploration Corps Space Vehicle Command Centers that direct spacecraft operations while Fleet Operations and Engineering Corps are in charge of spacecraft technology functions, mechanical engineering, communications, spacecraft computers, and robotic systems.

The first launches, from Cape Canaveral and Cape Wrath, delivered manned construction and utility spacecraft to the Moon's surface. Within two days, all spacecraft landed safely within the Cabeus crater to construct ASERA's first moon base.

In 2051, Moon base Cabeus was established. Under the Exploration Corps, its primary function is to drill deep in the shadows of the crater for ice, which occurs as a result of meteorite impacts, to obtain useable water, breathable oxygen, and hydrogen to fuel spacecraft. Moon base life support is maintained by converting mined ice into potable water and breathable oxygen, and by solar power obtained via special exterior paneling. The base is under the command of Captain Scott Baker, a former NASA astronaut and retired US Naval officer. Previously, Baker served as a supervising consultant for ASERA at Cape Canaveral during transitional operations. While an admiral had yet to be named, Baker also acts as the highest ranking member of the Exploration Corps for the time being. Terrell regards Baker as a well-qualified candidate for admiral, and Baker remains one until ASERA would later make its selection.

ASERA, as a private corporation, is not required to operate with transparency. When pressed by media outlets to divulge its plans, ASERA maintains its intention for drilling is to obtain usable water to support a self-sustaining system that would, perhaps, introduce new missions to Mars.

At Cabeus base, drilling robots operate at ten-hour intervals. Less than a year in operation, while drilling 31 kilometers through the regolith-rich crust, an abundance of platinum group metals were discovered.

Prior to ASERA's formation, Terrell and Dr. Westbrook had already caucused with the incoming board members to finalize confidential plans to extract an abundance of platinum group metals hidden within the Moon's crust. Their plan estimates that the Moon has more platinum than the Earth, resulting from billions of years of asteroid and comet impacts. Once the plan was finalized, the total investment was estimated at approximately $50 billion. Return projections would be approximately $100 billion annually in lunar platinum.

As corporate returns were being realized, additional Moon bases were quickly planned. In 2053, investment into ASERA space exploration increases.

The SCU-9 *Peleus* was commissioned in 2054. The spacecraft designation is utility class. Its crew consists of sixteen members: a commanding officer, an executive officer, a first pilot, a second pilot, a science officer, an engineering officer, a second engineering officer, a communications specialist, a robotics officer, three craft technicians, a steward, an assistant steward, a senior medical officer, and a junior medical officer. Its size is 176.78 meters long, 68.27 meters wide, and 38.71 meters high. Its acceleration was clocked at 83,756 kilometers per hour. Its endurance is fourteen months between maintenance. Its escape system consists of two lifeboats. It was manufacturer in large part by Astrium-Thales Aerospace.

The *Peleus*, ASERA's first spacecraft, is also the first to feature a unique gravity control system created by Dr. Westbrook that allows crewmembers in space to function in a more Earthlike environment. With the use of electro-magnetic wave pulses emanating throughout the spacecraft, zero-g is countered by the artificial creation of normal Earth gravity, or one-g. Common gravity is created by these pulses that provide a common floor and ceiling with actual Earth-weight mimicking, or AWM. For crewmembers serving long missions, these pulses also enable a normal flow of fluids in the vestibular system within the inner ear that allow persons to obtain balance and gain awareness of a floor and ceiling even when such conditions are artificially created. The system creates a healthy physical environment that stabilizes blood volume, pushes bodily fluids downward, averts tissue and bone atrophy, and prevents space adaptation syndrome—all resulting from long voyages in zero-g conditions. Also, the system supports the psychological wellbeing of the crewmembers and inhibits confusion by providing them with a normal Earth gravity environment.

ASERA spacecraft life support is comprised of four separate but interactive systems: oxygen and ventilation (OVS) that include storage tanks and filtration scrubbers; energy (ECS) that include electrical systems, control systems such as temperature control and navigational control; emergency suits capable of sustaining life via independent life support—oxygen, temperature control, helmet lighting—used to allow a crewmember some time to a board lifeboat and escape; and, finally, individual lifeboat life support systems.

Spacecraft propulsion consists of two stages: a delivery system stage, or DSS, via chemical combustion that carries the spacecraft into Earth's orbit, which is eventually jettisoned after entering Earth's orbit, and an operational system stage, or OSS, via a chemical combustion of liquid oxygen and liquid hydrogen. The OSS is part of the orbital maneuvering system that allows the spacecraft to navigate in space and to land back on Earth. The manufacturer of the propulsion systems was Moog Corporation.

Lifeboat technology consists of individual advanced lifeboat modules, or ALMs. Each ALM accommodates up to nine crewmembers, and they are equipped with a cabin life support system and an on-board health maintenance facility. The propulsion system consists of thrusters that utilize chemical combustion technology. Its navigation systems, both manual and automated, enable the module to dock with any other spacecraft, as well as serve as a return and descent vehicle. At full capacity, the maximum endurance of each ALM is two months.

The *Peleus*, and each subsequent spacecraft, has a self-contained robot on board, or OCR. It serves as the physical manifestation of the spacecraft's computer system. It has the capability of communicating with the on-craft computer system as well as on-craft computer systems on other spacecraft. Humanoid in form, it stands at 1.8 meters high and weighs 86.2 kilograms. Its frame boasts an agile design with 60 degrees of freedom: 65 degrees of freedom hand, 75 degrees of freedom arm, five degrees of freedom pelvis, and eight degrees of freedom leg. Its face is featureless with the exception of two optical lenses as eyes. Its brain, located in its chest, contains the most-advanced artificial consciousness system and features a super algorithm that supports an automated awareness of its own existence. In its back is housed a 4.5 kilowatt per hour battery. Designed and manufactured by Boston Dynamics, the robots are programed to be curious, to protect life and, if needed, to fully operate in space. The initial driving force to create such robots was purely economic. NASA's Dexterous Robotics Lab sought to develop the highly-advanced OCR model from the Valkyrie Series 9 to accompany a single astronaut to Mars. Sending one astronaut rather than two would significantly cut costs and, by sending a robot that could independently communicate, it would offer the astronaut adequate company during the long mission.

By 2055, Moon base Tycho was established within the Tycho crater. With ASERA Commander Eileen Bower, a former NASA astronaut, in charge, drilling operations quickly commenced. In several months, a cache of platinum, as well as palladium, was discovered. The promise of economic return continues to be confirmed.

A book published in 2055, *Gray Rush: Space Privatization and the Moon Industry* by Martin P. Alcott, analyzed the high investment returns of lunar-mined platinum group metals, which were increasingly being used in high-tech products, chemistry, and jewelry. According to Alcott, in 1955, revenue that fed America's space race came from taxpayers and was motivated by the prospect of military conflict with the

Soviet Union. In 2055, however, revenue from ASERA's control of the Moon's resources was motivated by the prospect of economic dominance over China.

The SCU-11 *Hyperion* was commissioned in 2055. Like the *Peleus*, its designation is utility class. The crew complement and spacecraft size are the same as the *Peleus*. Its acceleration was clocked at 83,109 kilometers per hour. Its endurance is fourteen months between maintenance. Its escape system consists of two ALMs. Its chief manufacturer was Astrium-Thales.

ASERA, with strong purchasing power, takes the lead in all outer-space activities leaving the China National Space Administration as its only exploration competitor. China, which historically has more scientifically-literate people than the US and the EU combined, loses various top scientists and engineers motivated by profit to join ASERA. To expand its technologies, ASERA secures contracts with private aerospace developers and manufacturers in an environment of competitive bidding.

In 2056, Captain Scott Baker is promoted to admiral. At his promotion ceremony in Chicago, Baker pledges to support ASERA in its entrepreneurial and philanthropic pursuits.

That same year, ASERA reconstructs the ISS into a highly-advanced space station and commissions it as the SDS-2 *Hephaestus*. Its designation is a space docking station to service ASERA spacecraft that include the *Peleus*, *Hyperion*, and other spacecraft—some that have not yet been constructed. The overall shape of the station, much of it newly-constructed, resembles a semi-circle measuring 610 meters at it widest. While serving entirely in Earth's orbit, the *Hephaestus* operates with a crew of twenty-one: a commanding officer, an executive officer, a pilot, a commanding science officer, a senior engineering officer, three engineering officers, a robotics officer, and twelve station technicians. Its endurance is ten years between maintenance. Its escape system consists of eight ALMs. Its chief manufacturer was Astrium-Thales Aerospace.

In the following year, both the Indian Space Research Organization, in Bangalore, and the Japan Aerospace Exploration Agency, in Tokyo, are acquired by ASERA. Also, Moon base Crisis is established as a research and drilling base. Admiral Baker arrived aboard the *Hyperion* to initiate base operations. The event was purely ceremonial.

In 2059, two more research and drilling Moon bases were established, Tranquility and Serenity. A year later, construction was completed on Moon base Fertility.

The SCT-27 *Artemion* was commissioned in 2061. The spacecraft designation is transport-freighter class. Its crew consists of sixteen members: a commanding officer, an executive officer, a first pilot, a second pilot, a senior engineering officer, two engineering officers, a navigation officer, a second navigation officer, a robotics officer, and six craft technicians. Its size is 340.67 meters long, 211.41 meters wide, and 92.39 meters high. Its acceleration was clocked at 76,719 kilometers per hour. Its endurance is twenty months between maintenance. Its escape system consists of six ALMs. It was manufactured in large part by Lockheed Martin. A year later, a second ship of this kind, the SCT-29 *Gigantes* was commissioned.

Meanwhile, the China National Space Administration experienced great difficulty on its own to commence drilling and mining operations. China was not a signer of the Outer Space Treaty of Monaco in 2041 and, before President Ming's death in 2062, he secretly expressed regret that his nation failed to keep up with ASERA's accomplishments. Former-President Richmond and former-Prime Minister Millington, while attending Ming's funeral, shared a conversation about the increase of wealth each of their nations shared as a result of allowing lunar mining operations.

\* \* \*

In 2068, the Goldstone Observatory in San Bernardino, California, tracked Asteroid 2048 MQ57, a C-type asteroid, and learned that they grossly miscalculated its trajectory. Its approach from the direction of the Sun rendered it temporarily invisible to Earth observers. Rather than passing a sizable distance away as previously estimated, when its path was reacquired, it was determined to be on an intercept course with Earth. At a total estimated size of two kilometers across, it has the potential of causing considerable destruction if it does indeed strike. Due to its massiveness, it was determined to be too large to effectively redirect. Its estimated arrival time will be sometime before the end of the century. Goldstone also reports that asteroid near encounters in general are on the rise.

During that same year, asteroid-finding telescope Sentinel-2 launched in 2051 by the B612 Foundation failed to detect Asteroid 2048 MQ57 due to a gradual compromise to satellite's thermal shields and a sudden malfunction of its antenna turret.

Before his death in 2071, Dr. Westbrook warned Terrell that planet Earth was in great peril. With concern for Terrell's son, Marcus, he pleaded with him that time was running out. In his last years, he finalized work on the Exodus Program. Terrell secretly regarded it as his old friend's swansong while he kept the work entirely confidential.

For now, Terrell ordered a new mission underway to destroy the asteroid. Although he has all the funding and resources at his disposal, he felt alone and anxious without Dr. Westbrook.

# Chapter One

The year is 2078. Aboard the *Cerberus*, a utility class spacecraft, we are in deep space— approximately 90 million kilometers from Earth and bearing down on Asteroid 2048 MQ57.

"Approach speed?" Culpepper asked while harnessed to the commander's chair.

"We're nearing top acceleration—83,981 kilometers per hour," answered Talbot. "We should be acquiring visual range in eighteen minutes."

"My estimation is sixteen minutes, thirty-seven seconds," Devol said.

"Kiss-ass robot," Talbot retorted with a snicker. "Which of your buttons makes coffee?" he asked rhetorically.

"Steady, Talbot," Cutler ordered.

Culpepper looks down at the flight instrument readout. "Maintain intercept course."

The SCU-14 *Cerberus*, manufactured in large part by Astrium-Thales Aerospace, was commissioned in 2056. Its crew of sixteen have been in space, thus far, for five months. The ship's space endurance allows it to remain for nine months more until its next maintenance docking at the *Hephaestus*. For this mission, the *Cerberus* systems were specially retrofitted for deep-space navigation.

Aboard, the spacecraft is commanded by Captain Allard Culpepper. Although he is generally quite competent, he has become increasingly tense and unsure of himself during this mission. Serving as his second-in-command is Commander Ronald Cutler— an arrogant ivy-leaguer who spent this mission second-guessing Culpepper's every step.

At the helm, Lieutenant Commander Henry Malcolm Talbot serves as first pilot. He was recruited directly from the EU Air Force to serve on the *Cerberus* because of his flying abilities and his fearlessness. Thus far, he has found this mission a bit incongruous as he witnesses heated exchanges on the bridge between Culpepper and Cutler. To amuse himself, Talbot interacts with OCR Devol, the *Cerberus'* on-craft robot.

The spacecraft's lethal payload consists of two nuclear devices each with an explosive package with the equivalent of five-hundred kilotons of TNT. The mission requires the *Cerberus* to jettison one of the warheads, engage its engines and travel to the asteroid so it may carefully attach itself to its surface. Then, the spacecraft must obtain a safe distance of two-hundred kilometers and then detonate the payload. Upon detonation, the asteroid should be fragmented sending small bits outward while disrupting the trajectory of any remaining remnants.

"Captain, we are now acquiring visual range," Talbot said.

"One-quarter speed," Culpepper ordered.

"One-quarter speed," Talbot repeated.

With each passing minute, the asteroid appears brighter in the window.

"There's the son of a bitch," Cutler said.

"Bring us to thirty kilometers," Culpepper ordered.

"Thirty kilometers," Talbot repeated.

"That's a bit close, captain," Cutler said.

Culpepper turns to him. "I want to get as close as possible and eliminate any room for error. We have only two chances to get this right."

"Even if it jeopardizes the ship," Cutler protests.

"All of humanity is depending on us to get it right. My order stands."

As the *Cerberus* approaches the asteroid, Culpepper carefully inspects its oblong shape and various craters.

"Devol, analysis," he ordered.

"One point two nine seven eight kilometers in diameter," Devol said. "Composition consists of eighty-six percent iron-nickel alloy. Minerals include carbon and silicon with trace amounts of organic compounds. It is a solid body. Speed is twenty-one point seven three nine kilometers per second and is rotating at a speed of point seven kilometers per second."

Culpepper presses a button on the instrument readout and speaks into a small microphone.

"Kirby, ready the package for jettison," he said.

*"Ready the package—aye, sir,"* is heard over a small speaker.

Culpepper then orders the communication channel open.

"Cerberus to ASERA mission command, over."

*"ASERA mission command, Cerberus,"* is heard over the speaker.

"Cerberus is on the approach to 2048 MQ57. We are preparing package for jettison."

*"Roger that, Cerberus. On the approach and preparing for jettison."*

"We are at thirty kilometers, Captain," Talbot said; "maintaining distance."

*"Package ready, sir."*

"Jettison on my mark. Nine, eight, seven..."

Cutler stares intensely out of the window while Talbot is joined by the second pilot.

"Where's my coffee, asshole?" Talbot asked the pilot somewhat playfully. "Captain's firing the package."

"...three, two, one."

The spacecraft jettisons the package.

*"Package jettison complete."*

"Engage the engines on my mark, Talbot. Nine, eight, seven..."

Talbot takes hold of a throttle. When the count reaches "one," Talbot pushes the throttle forward.

"Engines burning, sir," Talbot said.

"Roger that," Culpepper responded.

While the package is en route and nearly at its target, a huge flare illuminates the entire window. *Cerberus* experiences a dramatic vibration.

"What happened?" Culpepper ordered.

The spacecraft then shifts violently. Cutler, who was not fully harnessed into his seat, is thrown against the wall with such force that he is knocked unconscious. Talbot orders Devol to buckle Cutler back into his chair. But Devol just looks at him.

"Do it!" Talbot commands.

Another violent jolt sends the robot into the ceiling putting it out of commission. Talbot quickly opens his harnesses, grabs Cutler and straps him in. He then notices the second pilot attempting to harness himself only to see him slam his head on the controls. Talbot straps him in before returning to his chair.

After Talbot is harnessed, he answers Culpepper.

"Sir, the payload exploded," he said.

"How can that happen?" Culpepper demanded.

"I don't know, sir," Talbot answered while struggling to regain control of the spacecraft. Culpepper can only express a blank look.

*"ASERA mission command to Cerberus, what's going on up there? We're getting some serious readings here."*

Culpepper continues to convey a blank look.

"Captain!" Talbot said. "Captain?" Talbot speaks into his microphone. "ASERA, the package detonated prematurely, and the spacecraft is out of control. We are attempting to stabilize."

*"Roger that, Cerberus. Attempting to stabilize. What is the status of 2048 MQ57?"*

"Unknown at this time, mission command. Will advise."

Talbot engages the spacecraft's engines only to learn that the inertia cancelling system has been damaged.

"Helmets on!" Culpepper ordered. "Make ready the lifeboats!"

"That may not be necessary, sir," Talbot said.

Talbot open his harness and leaps to one of the wall panels. He quickly opens it and grabs a lock of multi-colored wiring.

"Captain, depress the valve switch and draw the throttle downward and hold it there."

Talbot pulls out a pocket knife, cuts a few wires, and connects two of them together. A rattling sound emanates from the engines. He then jumps back into his chair and buckles in.

"Okay, captain, let the throttle go now!"

As soon as Talbot takes the throttle, he begins to steadily take control of the spacecraft. Culpepper takes a deep breath. He speaks into the microphone.

"Kirby, status report?" he commanded. He turns back to Talbot. "How's Cutler?"

"He's alive," Talbot answered. "Concussion, maybe."

The second pilot begins to regain consciousness.

"You're okay, buddy?" Talbot asked him.

"What happened?" he asked.

"We experienced a shimmy."

"Some shimmy. My head mega-hurts."

"Senior medical officer to the bridge," Culpepper announced into the microphone. He takes another deep breath. "Good work, Talbot." He looks down at Devol on the floor; he then notices its severed head in the corner. "What is the status of the asteroid?"

"It was not fragmented, sir," Talbot said. "Computer scan indicates that it has been split into two irregular masses."

"Its trajectory?" Culpepper asked.

"Unknown at this time. The debris is hindering a full analysis. We may be able to jettison the other payload and detonate it to make certain."

"That may take too much time, and we need to hurry home. Besides, it looks fragmented," declared Culpepper. He then speaks into the microphone.

"Cerberus to ASERA mission command," he said.

*"ASERA mission command, go ahead Cerberus."*

"The payload detonated before it could attach itself and before the Cerberus could move far enough away. The spacecraft may have experienced serious damage—a status report is in the works. We have some injuries. 2048 MQ57 broke up, but we are unable to determine its trajectory due to the debris field surrounding it. We're returning to the Hephaestus. We will advise further. Cerberus, out."

*"Roger, Cerberus. You're heading home."*

"Captain, let's jettison the second package," Talbot advised.

"It's over, Talbot. The asteroid is destroyed as far as I'm concerned. Let's head for home."

\* \* \*

After six months, the *Cerberus* docks with the *Hephaestus*. All aboard survive the mission and, by this time, all injuries have healed—with the exception of Talbot's ego. Devol is repairable.

Concerns arise regarding Culpepper's actions while in command. But, a special tribunal clears him of any wrongdoing. The mission mishap is deemed a "system malfunction," and that there was a defect in the package's propulsion system. Culpepper retires.

For his heroic actions, Talbot is immediately promoted to commander. After a long vacation, he is reassigned to serve aboard the *Cerberus* this time as the executive officer.

Meanwhile, ASERA continues to monitor the remains of Asteroid 2048 MQ57, now designated

2048 MQ57a and 2048 MQ57b, to determine whether or not it remains a threat to Earth. What is known is that 2048 MQ57a is smaller and is traveling considerably faster than 2048 MQ57b, which is traveling behind it in the same path. For some time, the Goldstone Observatory loses sight of 2048 MQ57a. It momentarily reacquires it, but confuses it with 2048 MQ57b. Both disappear behind the Sun rendering them undetectable. Eventually, ASERA shifts their attention back to mining operations on the Moon with additional plans to re-start Mars expeditions with mining possibilities there.

It is believed that both 2048 MQ57a and 2048 MQ57b will miss Earth.

# Chapter Two

A summer's day in 2083, and all is in attendance in the center of ASERA's corporate plaza to honor Admiral Baker's retirement. Talbot, dressed in his class "A" uniform, stands at attention at the lavish ceremony. Baker, upon seeing Talbot, walks over to him. Talbot renders a salute.

"It sucks out there in space," Baker said. He returns the salute.

"You know it does, sir," Talbot returned.

"Well, it's a lot safer than being behind a desk in an office building, I assure you."

Talbot smiles.

"Which is why, my friend," Baker continues, "as my last official act I am promoting you to captain. You will command the *Hyperion*."

"Thank you?"

"Young man, did you join for exploration? For fun? A little of both? ASERA has made us rich. What's wrong with that? What's wrong with becoming even wealthier? You will report to Cape

Wrath on Monday, nine-hundred hours. A shuttle will take you to the *Hephaestus* where your ship awaits. Godspeed, Hank."

"Good luck, Scott."

* * *

After three years of supervising mining operations, Captain Talbot submits his retirement papers. A newly-purchased mansion set high on the hills overlooking Bristol Channel stands as his next "assignment."

"Captain, we have a hull breach! We're venting oxygen and we're losing gravity control! We need zone four shutdown! We need containment! Captain? Captain, please *answer!*"

Talbot wakes in his bed with a gasp. The covers fly off as he quickly sits up.

"Honey? Are you all right?"

"Yes, yes! I'm fine," Talbot said to his wife while rising.

"Coffee?" she asked.

"Please," he said while he pandiculates.

* * *

It is the morning of January 1, 2091. While wearing a warm robe and drinking gourmet coffee out of a mug sporting the ASERA logo, Talbot gazes out of his panoramic windows overlooking the blue waters. The rocky coast below reminds him of his dangerous past. He wonders how he survived it. In his head, he can still hear his sons playing out back even though they have grown and went off to college.

It's been four years since he retired. Yet, he still hasn't fully relaxed—like there was unfinished business.

* * *

The phone rings.

"Honey, it's for you."

Talbot presses a button on a control panel.

"Henry, it's me, Dan."

"Hey, Dan? Back on Earth?"

"Yeah. Um, I have some information that has not been released to the press yet. It's about the asteroid."

"Hold on, let me put you on headset." He puts it on. "Okay, go ahead."

"It has reappeared, and it's not good. Earth's gravity manipulated its path. Hank, it's on a collision course. It's too close for us to do anything."

"Which one?"

"MQ57a."

"And, the other?"

"It's hard to tell. The Sun's glare is making it difficult to track."

"How long?"

"One month, maybe two. The other, if it's on a collision course, a year?"

"Where does it look like MQ57a will strike?"

"Based on its speed and the Earth's rotation, Australia? Africa? It's big, Hank. You probably should stay put."

* * *

On February 4, Asteroid 2048 MQ57a, with an approximate diameter of eight-hundred sixty meters, struck off the coast of Madagascar, twenty-two degrees south latitude and sixty-seven degrees east longitude, at a speed of ninety-one kilometers per second striking with an impact force equivalent to twenty-two hundred megatons of TNT. It smashes into the Earth's atmosphere perpendicularly with little breakup and with severe and unrelenting ferocity. The shockwave in the trail of the asteroid is devastating.

Tons of ejections from the impact zone thrust upward with sufficient speed to escape the Earth's gravitation. Smaller meteorites either burn up in the atmosphere or rain back down on the Earth. Ocean wave heights reach forty-eight meters. Waves traveled, at most, forty kilometers inland.

The death toll in Madagascar is 33.12 million, in South Africa, 88.91 million, and Somalia reached 14.89 million. In India, 3.38 million were killed in Kozhikode, and 7.91 million were killed in Trivandrum. Thailand experienced 59.36 million killed. The Indonesian Islands reached 378.16 million. On the western coast of Australia, 10.94 million were killed. The Indian Ocean islands and atolls were completely destroyed where an estimated one-million people lived.

Asteroid 2048 MQ57a killed an estimated 597,608,531 people.

In the asteroid's aftermath, landmasses received vast destruction resulting from tidal waves radiating from the point of impact. Millions were unable to evacuate in time, and medical teams are unable to reach the injured. Rescue and relief efforts in coastal and island regions are lethargic and limited. Death was so sudden that surviving nations along the impact zones receive relatively few refugees.

The strike also obliterated ecological systems and disrupted food sources. For several weeks, regions surrounding the impact zone experiences thick, ash rainfall and strong winds, especially in Malaysia and Indonesia.

\* \* \*

Talbot is recalled by ASERA as an advisor on Asteroid 2048 MQ57b. ASERA believes the asteroid will miss. Talbot disagrees, but his analysis is in the minority opinion. As a result, Terrell decides to hold off on any mission to intercept and destroy it. As Talbot openly protests ASERA's decision and while he volunteered to head a search-and-destroy mission, he makes a new enemy in Terrell. Frustrated, Talbot returns to his home in Scotland.

\* \* \*

Nearly two years later, Asteroid 2048 MQ57b, with an approximate diameter of one thousand, one-hundred thirty meters, struck in the northern Pacific Ocean, thirty-two degrees north latitude and one-hundred sixty-nine degrees east longitude, at a speed of seventy-nine kilometers per second. It strikes with an impact force equivalent to forty-seven hundred megatons of TNT. Just as the smaller portion that struck, it smashes into the Earth's atmosphere perpendicularly. The shockwave in the trail of the asteroid is even more devastating than the previous strike.

Pollution in the form of a plastic "soup" vortex concentrated in the central-northern Pacific was ejected into the atmosphere and incinerated almost immediately. Tidal wave heights reached as high as eighty-seven meters. Waves traveled, at most, seventy kilometers inland.

Hawaii was obliterated, 1.5 million killed. The US west coast, especially California, was destroyed, 41 million killed. Southern portions of Alaska was wiped clean, 891,545 killed. The western Canadian coast, British Columbia, experienced 6.2 million killed.

Eastern Russia, at the Sea of Okhotsk, 676,986 were killed. Other areas in Russia include the Kamchatka Peninsula where 489,647 were killed, and the Magadan Oblast coast where 187,339 were killed.

Japan suffered heavy destruction, 94 million killed. South Korea was equally destroyed, 28 million killed. North Korea experienced a government overthrow in the aftermath. It is believed that 19 million lost their lives.

The total dead in China is 229 million. By province, in Jilin, 19 million were killed; in Liaoning, 29 million; Shandong, 68 million; Jiangsu, 71 million; and Zhejiang, 42 million killed.

Other Pacific islands suffered catastrophic loses, including the Philippine Islands with 112.74 million killed, Papua New Guinea with 9.98 million killed, and the Indonesian Islands with 207.39 million killed.

The eastern coast of Australia lost 20.87 million.

Asteroid 2048 MQ57b killed an estimated 772,873,149 people.

In the aftermath of this asteroid, mass destruction of landmasses resulted from ocean waves. Island evacuations were practically nonexistent. Thousands of coastal cities and towns were annihilated. Cities were devastated and left in ruins, tangled and twisted. Millions were unable to evacuate in time, and medical teams were unable to reach the injured. The scale of the disaster and challenges of delivering the assistance left many without help. Huge areas were strewn with debris and corpses. Hundreds of thousands of survivors were camped out at airports. There was little to no organized delivery of food, water, or medical supplies. There were difficulties with logistics. Survivors went too long without access to clean water, food, shelter and medical help. Disease broke out and thousands of people died as a result of wounds sustained during the destruction.

The asteroid strike was too swift for resources to manage. Damaged roads and other infrastructure issues complicated relief efforts. As the result of no electricity, rescue and relief planes couldn't land at disaster zones at night. There is also growing concern about recovering rotting corpses.

Food sources are scarce; refugees move inland to establish settlements where food is shipped and distributed.

Most affected areas experience almost constant rainfall; the weather in other areas of the world encountered asteroid dust clouds and experienced ash rainfall for nearly one month freezing crops and halting much of commerce.

However, the Earth is still largely habitable. Much of the world consumes genetically-engineered produce that seem to be resilient to the diminished sunlight. Gradually, people in surviving nations who brave the aftermath, and who remain industrious and optimistic, gradually move into decimated areas to clear and rebuild. In the decades that follow, upon newly-drawn coastal landscapes, civilizations experience a rebirth.

Localized industry reappears. Economic systems recover, and both the political and corporate worlds adopt strategies to preserve human life. The corporate leaders reinvest profits to grow the economy.

Emmett Terrell stands as one of those pioneers for rebuilding and regrowth. But, before he witnesses a full recovery, he dies in 2098. His son, Marcus, is swiftly appointed as the new chairman of ASERA. The young Terrell continues his father's legacy by assisting in reconstruction efforts. A world in turmoil is, as he puts it, "bad for business."

In a ceremony to honor his father, he names the Chicago headquarters complex the Emmett Terrell Center. Within that same month, a monument is erected in the plaza to honor the 1.37 billion killed by Asteroid 2048 MQ57 and its aftermath. It reads: "WHAT YOU LEAVE BEHIND IS NOT WHAT IS ENGRAVED IN STONE, BUT WHAT IS WOVEN INTO THE LIVES OF OTHERS – PERICLES."

* * *

In 2109, the Goldstone Observatory discovers another asteroid, 2027 RH211, moving at great speed—approximately ninety kilometers per second.

Based on their analysis, its estimated size is thirty kilometers in diameter, and that this mass may be headed toward Earth. They further estimate that it has a low probability of striking. For some time, Terrell receives details of its path while the information is kept from the public.

# Chapter Three

It is the summer of 2115, and Talbot, while aboard his luxury yacht, navigated to his favorite fishing spot. Although he always catches very few, he basks without a single care in the world. While pouring another drink, the phone rings.

"Dad, it's for you."

Talbot picks up.

"Hello?" he said.

"Hold for Mr. Terrell," his secretary said.

"Henry? It's me, Marcus."

"Hello, Marcus. How did you know it's my birthday?"

"I didn't. Actually, the reason why I'm calling is, well, let me be blunt."

Terrell conveys the details concerning Asteroid 2027 RH211.

"Henry, we're concerned that it may strike the Moon in a matter of months. Evacuation plans are underway while we assemble a team. I need you to lead it."

"Just shoot it out of the sky."

"We can't do that. It's too big and too close for that now. All we can do is get our people off the Moon and hope for the best."

"What do you need me to do?"

"I need you to report to the Cape Wrath launch base immediately. The base commander, Captain Andrew Barnes, will brief you on the details. While there, you'll assume the rank of admiral of the fleet. You will then be transported to the *Hephaestus* where your ship awaits. I'm sorry for the lack of pomp and circumstance."

"That's okay; I never liked that stuff anyway. What ship am I taking?"

"It's a new one, about to be commissioned. It's the SCE-7 Orpheus, and it still has that new-car smell."

"I'm on my way," Talbot said with a serious tone.

"And, admiral," Terrell pauses, "Thank you."

\* \* \*

Talbot naps while riding in his autocar. As it approaches Cape Wrath, a chirping alarm emits from its dash panel waking him before he reaches the base guardhouse.

While well inside the base grounds, he is greeted at the steps of the administration building.

"Welcome, admiral," Barnes said while extending his hand.

"Captain Barnes," Talbot said while taking his hand.

"Let's go to my office."

While inside, Talbot receives an encrypted digital attaché and a large garment box.

"Admiral, you may use my washroom to freshen up and change. Your launch is scheduled for one hour, so maybe you should get a bite to eat. I'll send for the steward."

"Just coffee."

On a small launch pad, the S-5 *Eagle* is prepped for launch. This small, shuttle class spacecraft sports the triangular-shaped ASERA logo on its fuselage. Manufactured by Boeing, it is designed to enter Earth's orbit to rendezvous with space stations and larger spacecraft. It has an acceleration of 70,989 kilometers per hour with an endurance of twenty-two hours between maintenance. Its crew consists of two crewmembers: a first pilot and a second pilot.

\* \* \*

While wearing his admiral's uniform and while holding his ASERA mug, Talbot makes his way to Pad Four-E. He passes technicians who pause from working to stand at attention as he walks by.

"Please don't let me interrupt you," he said to them.

As Talbot sees the S-9 *Comet* and the S-11 *Horizon* being worked on, he asks a technician a general question while not expecting a specific answer.

"So, how's it going?"

"Admiral, I swear, these shuttle class spacecraft suck!" the technician said.

"In what way?"

"The launch engines leak excessively." He points to the main fuel valve at the thrust chamber. "See?"

"Yes, I see." Talbot said slowly.

"I don't know how they are able to enter Earth's orbit," he said just before he walked off.

Talbot takes a quick swig from his mug.

"Try bubblegum," he said.

\* \* \*

"...seven, six, five, engine ignition, three, two, one."

The spacecraft rumbles as it lifts off.

*"Eagle, you have cleared the tower,"* is heard in their helmets.

"Copy that, Wrath."

The spacecraft pierces the stratosphere.

"Welcome aboard, admiral," the first pilot said. "Our ETA is three and a half hours, so enjoy the ride."

Talbot looks through his window at the Moon and sees the base settlement lights. It appears as though the Moon is inhabited with tiny cities. As the spacecraft rolls, Talbot looks back at Earth. He ponders the notion of two Earths and, perhaps, three if the Mars program is ever revived.

In two hours, the *Hephaestus* is in sight.

"Hephaestus, Eagle initiating docking procedures."

*"Copy that, Eagle. Hephaestus is ready to receive you,"* the communications officer confirmed.

As the shuttle pitches, Talbot views several docked spacecraft, including a newer behemoth.

\* \* \*

The welcoming party consists of commanders of each spacecraft of the entire fleet. Out front is Captain Ian Carmichael, *Hephaestus* commander.

"Admiral, welcome!" Carmichael said.

"Thank you. Hello, all! Before, I tour my ship and get situated, we need to gather around a very big table."

"Admiral, let's reconvene in my conference room in the lower deck. There's plenty of room there."

"I want all base commanders hailed and on a live feed uplink to that room in ten minutes," Talbot directed.

"Yes, admiral."

\* \* \*

In the *Hephaestus* conference room, all of the various commanders are seated around a huge table and are engaged in informal conversation with one another. For many of them, it is a reunion of sorts from prior military services. Large screens are mounted high on every wall. Displaying on most of them are moon base commanders getting settled into their seats.

Carmichael enters and calls the room to attention. Talbot then enters and, before he takes a seat at the head of the table, he orders the assembly to be seated.

"Colleagues, the Moon is faced with a crisis. And we've been asked to evacuate the Moon bases of all ASERA personnel."

Talbot looks up at the screens and directs each Moon base commander to report.

"Captain Steven Wilcox, Cabeus."

"Commander Ronald Meade, Tycho."

"Commander Alan Young, Crisis."

"Commander Mikhail Kadnikov, Tranquility."

"Commander Edward Liang, Serenity."

"Commander Eileen Bower, Fertility."

"Commanders," Talbot said, "You will prepare your personnel and equipment for departure. You will pack all of your command effects and logs. You will do this within forty-eight hours. Commanders of the utility class spacecraft report."

"Captain Mamoru Mukai, SCU-9 Peleus."

"Captain Curt Mitchell, SCU-11 Hyperion."

"Captain Ellie Briscoe, SCU-14 Cerberus."

"Hi, folks." Talbot looks down at his digital attaché. "The Peleus will evacuate Tycho. The Hyperion will evacuate Crisis. The Cerberus will evacuate Tranquility." He looks up. "And, the Orpheus will evacuate Cabeus. Commanders of the transport-freighter class spacecraft report."

"Captain Leonid Levchenko, SCT-27 Artemion."

"Captain Bruce Pettit, SCT-29 Gigantes."

"The Artemion will evacuate Serenity. The Gigantes will evacuate Fertility."

Talbot looks at Pettit. "I can't help but notice that—a man with your name—is commanding the Gigantes."

The room erupts with laughter.

"Bruce," Talbot adds, "just because you served in the EU Air Force does not mean you'll get any special privileges from me."

The laughter continues.

"I wouldn't think of it, admiral," Pettit said with a smile.

"After the fleet evacuates all Moon bases, it will rendezvous and dock with the Hephaestus and wait out the strike. Any questions?"

* * *

After adjournment, Talbot engages in a private conversation with Briscoe.

"Ellie, it's been so long."

"Admiral."

"C'mon, Ellie, no one's listening."

She smiles. "Henry," she said.

"I was happy to learn that you took command of the Cerberus. I read about it in the London Times."

"Is that what you really want to talk about?" she asked with a slight smile.

"Ellie, things got complicated. I was in space more than I anticipated. The truth is, I never stopped thinking of you."

"I'm sure Alison would be glad to know that," she said sarcastically.

"We divorced. It's been four years."

Briscoe thinks for a moment. "And now here we are."

"Now here we are." Talbot looks into her eyes.

"Good luck, captain." He smiles.

"Thank you, admiral. Good luck." She smiles back, turns, and walks to dock seven to board her spacecraft.

"Just as I remembered her," Talbot said to himself.

* * *

At dock four, Talbot enters the SCE-7 *Orpheus* to tour the spacecraft. Therein, the entire spacecraft's company of twenty-four crewmembers are standing at attention in inspection formation.

"Admiral on board!" the executive officer announced. He turns to Talbot. "Welcome aboard the Orpheus. We are prepared for you to take command, Admiral Talbot."

"Captain Samuel Kendrick, I look forward to working with you." Talbot shakes his hand. "I knew your father—outstanding military leader. You've had some shoes to fill. How is the old chap?"

"Dead, sir."

"Oh, I'm sorry to hear that."

Talbot and Kendrick briefly inspect the crewmembers. In attendance is the first pilot, the second pilot, the senior science officer, the junior science officer, the engineering officer, the second engineering officer, the communications specialist, the navigation officer, the second navigation officer, four spacecraft technicians, the steward, the assistant steward, the chief medical officer, two senior medical officers, the senior spacecraft cadet, and two spacecraft cadets.

The engineering officer, Commander Lowell Cooper, joins Talbot and Kendrick for the tour of the spacecraft.

"The spacecraft designation is exploration class—the first of its kind," Cooper said. "Unlike the utility class spacecraft, its design allows for interplanetary travel. It was initially conceived in anticipation of a renewed Mars manned exploration program. It's a fitting flagship, sir, I assure you."

"Thank you, commander," Talbot said. "We will depart to Cabeus base in two hours."

"Yes, sir. And, please call me Coop. Everyone else does."

"Thank you, Coop," Talbot said with a smile.

Kendrick resumes the tour by leading Talbot to the technician's section of the spacecraft adjacent to the rear hanger. As they pass a number of space-to-surface probes with their innards exposed, Talbot sees something of interest out of the corner of his eye. Unlike those he encountered in his long career with ASERA, this one is the most advanced he has ever seen. He steps up to it while Kendrick follows close behind.

"Admiral, this is the Orpheus' on-craft robot, OCR Tesla," Kendrick said.

"Tesla, what can you tell me about the Orpheus?" Talbot asked.

"Exploration class, interplanetary. Its size is two-hundred fifty-one point forty-six meters in length, one-hundred thirty point seventy-six meters in width, and eighty-five point sixty-four meters in height. Its chief manufacturer is Astrium-Thales Aerospace. Top acceleration is eighty-five thousand, seven hundred eighty-six point twenty-three kilometers per hour. Endurance is twenty-eight months between maintenance. Its escape system consists of four ALMs, two forward and two aft..."

"Stop," Talbot ordered. "Impressive."

"It's a pleasure to meet you, admiral," Tesla continues. "Your entire career has been downloaded into my system database and—if I may say—I find it... *impressive*," Tesla said.

"Kiss ass!" a man said from behind the robot. The man then emerges.

"Oh, and allow me introduce your robotics officer, Lester Malachy," Kendrick said.

"Admiral, it is an honor." They shake hands.

"Malachy. Our dads knew one another."

"Yes, I believe they did. Your father was Captain William Talbot—a hero pilot in the Royal Air Force who later served as the first chief marshal of the EU Air Force."

"Malachy, I called *your* dad 'Uncle Pete.' He was a remarkable scientist and innovator. In fact, he was the one who influenced me to leave the EU Air Force and join ASERA. Let me show you something."

Talbot takes his mug and sets it on the floor. He stands directly over the mug and carefully drops from his mouth a long line of sputum into it.

"If it wasn't for your dad, I would not be able to do that in a spacecraft in outer space," Talbot said with a smile.

"Would you mind if I pissed in it, sir?" Malachy said.

"Lester!" Kendrick said sternly.

"No, Kendrick, it's okay. Malachy, I bet you'd find it difficult to piss in front of an admiral."

Malachy thinks for a moment. "I'd rather have a drink with you, sir."

Talbot smiles. "Maybe after this is all over we'll do just that."

"Yes, admiral, I shall hope so." Malachy smiles back.

Talbot looks at Tesla again. This time, he looks at it up close.

"Malachy, you have your work cut out for you," he said. "Robot technology is something that I will never understand—especially in the area of artificial consciousness. So, tell me, does Tesla have a sense of humor?"

"Sir?" Malachy asked with a puzzling look.

Talbot turns and picks up his mug.

"Kendrick, let's go to the bridge. Malachy, it's been a pleasure."

"The pleasure was all mine," Malachy answered while the men walk away. When they are out of sight, his smile quickly escapes his face.

As the men make their way to the bridge, Kendrick offers his input.

"Before the robot could have a sense of humor, Malachy must upload one into himself."

"Copy that," Talbot said; "but I've always had respect for him and his family."

On the bridge, crewmembers hasten about to execute departure.

"Admiral on the bridge!" a crewmember called out.

The bridge, a long, rectangular space situated forward on the top deck, serves as the brain center of the spacecraft. All of the piloting, navigation, and control systems focus within and operate from this location. At the forward most, two chairs are occupied by the first pilot on the right and the second pilot on the left. Each have at their command numerous instruments, readouts, and steering systems. Behind them sit the engineering officer and the navigation officer and, behind them sit two spacecraft technicians serving as system specialists. The executive officer and commanding officer occupy chairs at the rear. Surrounding the bridge on all sides, fluorescent light aluminates from in between a multitude of panels that house various switches and knobs. Talbot sits in the commanding officer's chair. Before he buckles in, he proceeds to enter data into a keypad on his panel.

While crewmembers labor to get the spacecraft underway, Kendrick calls out to the second pilot.

"Anders, report." The young, slicked-back officer stands before Talbot. "This is Lieutenant Kenneth Anders. He will also be serving as our communications officer."

"A pleasure, sir," Anders said.

"The pleasure is mine. Go to your post."

As Anders moves toward his chair, Kendrick calls out to the first pilot.

"Fletcher, report."

A young, slender officer emerges from her chair and reports to the captain. Kendrick turns to Talbot.

"Admiral, this is our first pilot, Lieutenant Commander Joan Fletcher."

"Sir," Fletcher said to Talbot.

"Fletcher," Talbot said. "Pilots spend no special joy in walking."

"Sir?"

"Pilots like flying."

Fletcher displays a puzzled look.

"Neil Armstrong," Talbot said. "Ancient history?"

"Oh, no, sir. I understand."

"Good, a spacecraft is only as effective as its pilot. So, do your best or I'll have to kill you."

Talbot and Kendrick laugh while Fletcher offers a nervous smile.

"Ready us for departure. Let's push off."

Fletcher quickly returns to her chair. Anders speaks into his microphone.

"Hephaestus dock control, this is Orpheus. Ready to initiate departure procedure."

*"Roger that, Orpheus,"* is heard over the speaker. *"Ready for departure."*

All crewmembers take their chairs and report. The admiral receives an "all systems go" from each of them, and then he commences departure countdown. At zero seconds, the *Orpheus* docking mechanism detaches from the *Hephaestus*. The spacecraft's control thrusters are activated driving it away from the space station. After a few moments, Talbot orders main thruster burn.

* * *

The mission to evacuate all Moon bases was proceeding as planned. Aboard the *Orpheus*, Talbot receives ASERA personnel while he carefully supervises all evacuations.

The last Moon base evacuated is Cabeus. Before Captain Wilcox and two technicians board a rendezvous shuttle to take them to the *Gigantes*, they stand by a main power grid that supplies power to all Moon bases. They have a communication channel open with Talbot.

"Steve, I want you to access the master grid and commence power shutdown," Talbot ordered.

All Moon bases go dark.

\* \* \*

On a frigid January in 2116, Alexander M. Cox was sworn in as the 59th President of the United States. Marcus Terrell and his family sat prominently on the inaugural dais. During television coverage, pundits from various news syndicates referred to Al Cox as "the best president ASERA could buy." They ignore the fact that the corporation has also served as a top philanthropic global contributor.

Within his first week in office, Cox met with Emilio Busconi, the EU Prime Minister, and he shared a phone conversation with Hu Yang, the newly-elected president of China. More importantly, he met with Terrell to discuss the evacuations of the Moon bases and the after effects of the asteroid strike, if it should occur. Although both men had concern over the disruption to outer space commerce, Cox had additional concerns over the Moon's sustainability.

"I've known your father for many years, Marcus," Cox said. "He was a great American and a world-renown humanitarian. I know that you share the same concerns that he always had—concerns over our preservation, our survival. The world knows that ASERA will do its very best."

"We will do all we can, Mr. President."

\* \* \*

At a size of 34.7 kilometers in diameter, with a mass of one-one hundredth that of the Moon, Asteroid 2027 RH211 strikes the Moon at a speed of one-hundred kilometers per second. As a direct result, it speeds up the Moon's orbit and, at the same time, increases its trajectory away from Earth. After the debris cloud subsides it is learned that most of the Moon bases were destroyed. Fortunately, all bases were evacuated on time.

As the Moon's distance gradually increases, Earth begins to experience rotational instability. Without the Moon's gravitational pull, the Earth's rotation tumbles slightly. Weather patterns become extreme as tides and currents change dramatically. Eventually, in the final throes of their symbiotic relationship, the Moon will be set aloft on a path leading out of our solar system while Earth's rotational stability will be lost entirely. Our planet will become uninhabitable to most life. Mass extinctions will occur.

# Chapter Four

Moon bases Cabeus and Tycho have been spared from the asteroid's destruction. In a short time, their power is restored. Crisis, Tranquility, Serenity and Fertility bases, however, are all destroyed. Reconstruction is swiftly underway with a priority toward generating usable oxygen.

Soon after new, more advanced drilling robots—Mole Series 4—are in place at Cabeus and Tycho, their long arms easily extend deep within the Moon's crust. Due to shifts in the crust resulting from the asteroid strike, it took several attempts to reach concentrated ice clusters. When these clusters are located and accessed, oxygen production and storage gets well underway.

"Push it to forty-six kilometers," Captain Wilcox ordered.

The tri-cone drill bit penetrates the rock with considerable force. The entire drilling apparatus shakes violently.

At Tycho, Commander Meade is experiencing similar challenges. The *Artemion* needed to deliver a replacement drilling robot after the one they were using seized up. Although the Series 4 is said to be much more highly advanced than its predecessor, the Series 2, Meade sees very little difference.

* * *

Aboard the *Orpheus*, meanwhile, Kendrick is on the bridge monitoring refueling from the *Gigantes*. In just a few hours, the spacecraft will enter the Moon's orbit to allow Talbot to supervise operations on the far side. But, for now, there is little going on. Malachy enters the bridge.

"You wanted to see me, captain?" Malachy asked.

"I need Tesla to communicate with the computer to verify its order sequencing."

Just then, Cooper enters the bridge while holding a digital clipboard and whistling an indistinguishable tune.

"Coop! Another man I want to see," Kendrick said with a grin.

As the engineering officer, Commander Cooper's chief function is to program and maintain all mechanical systems on the spacecraft.

"The left stabilizers are not fully cooperating," Kendrick said. "If we didn't compensate with the right stabilizers, we'd drift away from the Gigantes. Talk to me."

"I thought I already fixed that problem, captain."

"Fletcher, tell me the thruster configuration numbers," Kendrick ordered.

"Seventy-twenty-ten, captain," Fletcher said.

"That can't be right," Cooper said.

"Of course not, commander. How can the numbers possibly be accurate?" Fletcher quipped with a tinge of sarcasm.

"Let me see your panel, lieutenant commander," Cooper ordered Fletcher. As he views the readouts, his face gradually relaxes. "Fletcher, it appears your numbers are accurate. Captain, how's the refueling going?"

"We're maintaining position—especially because Fletcher is such an outstanding pilot."

Fletcher looks at Kendrick and smiles.

While Kendrick turns, he unsuccessfully attempts to hide a grimace.

"Captain, what's wrong?" Cooper asked.

"I think I need to plug myself in," Kendrick answered while rubbing his neck.

"Oh, I see," Cooper said.

"Begging the captain's pardon, plug?" Malachy asked.

"The captain has a second brain," Cooper said to Malachy.

"Commander, I don't see the humor," Malachy quipped.

Kendrick faces Malachy.

"Lester, I sustained a spinal cord injury in my neck as a boy. I was paralyzed from the neck down." Kendrick gestures to his back. "A second brain was implanted here. It sends signals to electrode arrays that then activate nerves in my torso, arms and legs, which allow for voluntary movement and complete muscular control and mobility. The second brain enlists local motor circuits to find signaling paths to help initiate movement. So, you see, I'm half robot."

Malachy displays an annoyed look.

"Captain, may I have a word?" Cooper asked.

"Certainly, Coop." He turns to Malachy. "That will be all, commander."

Fletcher and Cooper proceed down a narrow hall. Cooper abruptly turns to Kendrick.

"Sam, I already addressed the thruster problem twice. I don't understand."

"Look, Coop, it's a new ship. Maybe it has some kinks that need to be ironed out."

"But, Sam, we're in outer space and about to embark on a lunar orbit. And, what the fuck's with Malachy? I asked him several times to sync the main computer with the navigational systems. He's not doing it, and I can't order him."

"Yeah, I don't know—there is something about him that leaves me with an uneasy feeling. I'll get back to you on that. In the meantime, repair the stabilizers after refueling, and then stay on top of it."

"Okay, Sam. We'll talk." Cooper turns to walk away, but not before saying something about Fletcher.

"She is hot."

"Coop, stabilizers."

\* \* \*

In the robotics shop, Malachy is testing some programs that were newly-installed into Tesla's mainframe. While working, he manages to retrieve a final spoonful of vegemite from the bottom of a small, plastic container.

"Tesla, run systems twelve through forty-one."

Tesla is seated on a workbench with its entire rear panel open. Its electro-mechanical grids are fully exposed and illuminating brightly. Its qualion chambers pulsate.

"Running..."

"Also, access ship's computer. How many jars of vegemite are recorded in the ration's manifest?"

"Accessing... Seven."

"Christ!"

"Systems run completed, commander. Shall I run systems forty-two through sixty-one?"

"Negative. Run diagnostic on power cell four. I think I may need to replace it."

Malachy is a G-9 ASERA employee. His designation is similar to that of a warrant officer with technical expertise. He holds the rank equivalent to a commander due to his seniority.

"What do you think of Fletcher?" Malachy asked.

"Running... I think she is a highly capable and well-seasoned pilot."

"Well, I don't trust her."

"Diagnostic complete. Power cell four needs replacement."

"I thought so." Malachy shifts in his chair. "Do you think Kendrick is fucking her? Run systems forty-two through sixty-one."

"Running... *Fucking?* Scanning..."

Malachy releases a deep belch and inserts a finger into his nose.

"Systems run completed." Tesla hesitates a moment. "By fucking, do you mean fornicating?"

"Yes, and any related activities. Continue scan."

"My scan does not indicate fortification or any related activities between Kendrick and Fletcher. However, I do indicate accelerated heart rate and an increase in skin temperature in Fletcher wherever Kendrick enters the bridge. These biological increases may be indicative to a precursor to fornication. Shall I run a fornication and related activities scan on any of the other crewmembers?"

"Negative. Hide scan and power down. I'll change your power cell after I sleep."

"Powering down. Sleep well, commander."

Tesla powers down while Malachy rises from his chair. He makes some last-minute log entries on a digital clipboard as the doorbell rings.

"Yes?" Malachy said.

"Technician Haise, sir," he said from behind the door.

"Come."

The spacecraft technician enters. "Sir, you are needed on the bridge by Captain Kendrick."

Malachy offers a groan. "Inform the good XO that I'm on my way."

"Right away, sir." The spacecraft technician leaves.

Malachy looks around the shop. "Not a happy place. Perhaps, I should introduce another stabilization issue for them to deal with."

\* \* \*

Among all of the strategies to draw the Moon closer, the plan with the least margin of error involves the placement of hundreds of thrusters on the Moon's far side. According to plan, the sustained thrust will slow the Moon's orbit and draw it closer to Earth. A follow-up mission, to be launched in some years, would aim to permanently stabilize the Moon's orbital position.

In 2118, two command bases are swiftly constructed for the sake of the mission. They include Moon base Eris 1 in the Cognitive Sea. It is under the command of Commander Mikhail Kadnikov, the former commander of Moon base Tranquility. The other is Moon base Eris 2 at the Kepler Crater Plateau. Commander Eileen Bower, the former commander of Moon base Fertility, serves as its commander. Several other bases are rapidly constructed on the Moon's far side to manage huge grids where thrusters and fueling systems are arranged.

* * *

Back aboard the *Orpheus*, Talbot is in his quarters. He is finishing a shower when the doorbell rings. He turns off the water.

"Yes?" he said.

"Breakfast, sir," the steward answered from behind the door.

"Okay, one moment."

Around Talbot's neck hangs an elongated, octagonal-shaped key attached to a chain. It swings as he grabs a white towel. He throws the towel over his back while he slides his feet into slippers and drapes on a robe. He opens the door.

"I'm sorry, sir," the steward said while holding a tray of food. "I can come back later."

"No, please. I'm starving. Just put it on the table."

Some papers are sprawled out on the table. Talbot quickly moves them out of the way.

"I'd give you a tip, but this isn't a cruise ship."

"Yes, sir." The steward smiles. "Will that be all?"

"Yes, thank you."

Talbot lifts the tray lid and sees something that resembles eggs, potatoes, and bacon. He can't help but grimace at the sight of it.

"I have a feeling that this is going to put the burgers on the *Hephaestus* to shame," he thinks.

Before returning to the bathroom, Talbot's eye catches something in the corner. Perched on a small table by the bed is a framed portrait of his father, James. As a career military man, the elder Talbot served as the EU Air Force general under Prime Minister Millington. He picks up the portrait. For some time, he hasn't given this image a careful look. As he gazes at his uniform, his medals, and his eyes, he wonders what his father would say about his accomplishments. He wonders if he would display pride. Probably not. He then thinks of his sons. As a career military man himself, he wonders whether or not he was a good father. He puts the portrait down.

After pouring himself a cup of coffee, he walks over to a large window and notices how the Moon's reflection shimmies off the side of the spacecraft.

# Chapter Five

The asteroid strike caused considerable damage. The aftermath includes a moderate shift in the Moon's ice crust. Surrounding the drilling bases, much of the crust is exposed. Through crevices, considerable amounts if ice crystals release into the lunar atmosphere. As a result, exhaustive operations are underway to conserve ice crystals and to create new wells. There is undisturbed ice to be found deeper within the crust. During the numerous attempts to locate ice, several drilling apparatuses become damaged forcing teams to drill many more wells than originally anticipated.

* * *

While Cabeus base vigorously drills, the bit strikes something hard—something large. The drilling robot cannot entirely classify the object as either ice or rock as the data is relayed to the drill team.

"All stop!" the supervising technician called out. "Lift the drill pipe!"

Down the drill hole, the technician sees a dark mass. He then sees movement.

"Focus some light down here, dammit!"

The apparatuses flood the hole with illumination.

"What the—! Notify the captain."

"Sir?" a team member asked.

"Notify the captain... *Now!*"

\* \* \*

Aboard the *Orpheus*, Malachy's doorbell rings.

"Who?"

"Talbot."

"Please come, admiral."

Talbot enters to find Malachy testing the dexterity of Tesla's left arm.

"Commander, do you have a moment?"

"Admiral, for you I have several. What may I do for you, sir?"

Talbot notices Tesla holding what appears to be an egg in its left hand. It is slowly raising it above its head.

"What is Tesla doing?" Talbot asked.

"Whatever I tell it to do."

"Is he going to break that egg?"

"If he does, he fails the test. Did you visit to talk about Tesla?"

"Sort of. I want to talk about Dr. Peter Malachy."

"Uncle Pete?"

"Your father, yes."

"What would you like to know?"

"He pioneered several important advancements in space technology. He gave us artificial gravity."

"The system's conscious interpretation of Earth's gravity on a spacecraft in outer space, yes," Malachy added.

"His work included artificial consciousness. May we speak in confidence?"

Malachy looks at him with a serious expression. "Certainly, admiral."

"Several years ago, I served aboard the *Cerberus*. OCR Devol hesitated to protect life when ordered. So, when it comes to robots, well, let's just say I have my doubts. How much did your father tell you about robot consciousness?"

"Standard computer functioning for robots includes computation and probability. The concept of robot consciousness, however, operates on a super-advanced algorithm that supports an artificial intelligence processor. This enables the robot to engage in logic and reasoning, allows it to have a capacity for learning, problem solve and plan, and maintain memory and recall. Beyond this threshold, the robot becomes aware of its own existence."

"I think therefore I am," Tesla interrupted.

"Is it capable of independent thought?" Talbot asked.

"Well, admiral, when Dr. Malachy created the first prototype for artificial consciousness, he included a capacity for primordial feelings to dramatically increase its range of emotions. After a few basic tests, the robot felt threatened and went on the attack. A technician was seriously injured before the robot could be physically restrained by four men. The prototype was aware of its physical environment, it could process stimuli, and it had a general perception of time and place. But, it was entirely unresponsive to questions and commands. It experienced a form of birth."

"It panicked," Talbot said.

"It was overcome by fear unexpectedly. Once a balance was struck in its programming between human emotion and advanced thought, its decision making capabilities became value-based, it gathered experiences and formulated values, and it became capable of resolving program conflicts autonomously. The prototype reported a sense of mental continuum—a moment-to-moment awareness. Sleep-wake cycles were integrated into its system. Eventually, its sense of selfhood generated feelings of love and admiration for music, art and, most importantly people. It developed a value for human life. And, it gained respect for authority and a sense of duty."

Malachy gestures toward Tesla's chest. "It's all in here," he said. "A system so large that it can't fit in the head. Improvements were then made to its physical dexterity and its reaction to the physical environment until we have what we see."

"So, what happened to Devol on that mission?"

"I don't know. Perhaps it was overwhelmed. Admiral, my father's original goal was not only to create a close-to-human counterpart for manned Mars missions. He wanted to create robotic supermen. Dr. Westbrook had other plans for the technology."

"ASERA," Talbot responded.

"I know that you're fond of my father's work. But, I know him differently. Although I was his only true human creation, I was nonexistent to him."

"Well, my father was not happy when I first joined ASERA. He called the commercialization of outer space the bastardization of human potential."

"And now, here we are together, sir," Malachy said with a grin.

"Here we are together," Talbot responded. "Should robots be programmed to exercise free will?"

"Autonomy for robots?" Malachy asked rhetorically.

"Will robots kill?"

"None have ever been programmed to kill—only to protect human life."

"Then how can we regard a robot as a conscious being?"

"That is the question, admiral." Malachy turns to Tesla. "Tesla, squeeze the egg."

"But, commander, if I break the egg I will fail the test."

"Tesla, the test involves following orders," Malachy said.

Tesla squeezes the egg. Its contents run down its arm.

"Admiral, is it free will or determinism? Is Tesla refusing orders? Is it merely requesting additional information?"

Talbot is about to answer.

*"Admiral to the bridge,"* Anders conveyed over the spacecraft's speaker system. *"Priority one."*

"I have to go, Lester. We'll talk more later."

"Looking forward to it, admiral."

Talbot swiftly makes his way.

\* \* \*

As Talbot entered the bridge, Kendrick rushes up to him.

"Admiral, we have received a communication from Captain Wilcox on Cabeus. He found something remarkable."

"Open communications with him," Talbot ordered.

"Open, sir," Anders said.

"Orpheus to Cabeus base, come in."

*"Admiral, you're not going to believe this,"* Wilcox said.

"Steve, try me. I'm all ears."

*"While we were drilling we hit a dark mass, something huge—maybe the size of a whale—deep inside the drill hole."* Wilcox hesitates. *"It appears to be an alien creature, sir."*

"Wha—? Is it alive?" Talbot asked.

*"No, sir. It appears to be dead."*

"Okay, Steve." Talbot turns to Fletcher. "Set us on a descending course to Cabeus. What is our ETA?"

"Nine hours, admiral," she said.

"Steve, the Orpheus will descend to Cabeus to investigate. We'll be there in about nine hours. In the meantime, do nothing to disturb the specimen and continue monitoring it."

*"Will do, admiral. We're standing by."*

"Right, Steve. See you soon." Talbot said. "Anders, end communication."

"Unbelievable!" Kendrick said.

"What is this thing?" Talbot said. "Is it a threat? Let's assemble in the conference room in five minutes. I want Malachy and Cooper. Let's come up with some procedures."

\* \* \*

In the conference room, Kendrick, Malachy, and Cooper anxiously await Talbot. Cooper is tapping his laser pen on his digital pad.

"So, ah, why is Fletcher so uptight?" he said.

"You're such a dick, Coop," Kendrick said.

"Let me get this right: we happen upon what could be the most astonishing discovery in the history of mankind and you're both harping over Fletcher?" Malachy asked sarcastically with a tinge of rhetoric. "But, while we're on the subject, captain, could we have recruited a more qualified pilot to serve on the fleet's flagship, or does she know someone in high places?" Malachy looks at Kendrick.

"She is well qualified, commander," Kendrick retorted. "Know your place, ol' chap."

Just before Malachy responds, Talbot enters the room. He clutches some photographs and documents. The three officers attempt to stand at attention.

"No, please," Talbot ordered while gesturing for them to remain seated. "Anders received some photographs from Cabeus of the underground anomaly." He passes them out.

"What the hell is it?" Cooper asked while looking at the image. "I don't see it."

"I do," Malachy said. "It appears to be an arachnid of some kind." He points to an area of the photograph. "Here is the torso, the legs, and the head, there."

"Okay, I see it," Talbot said. "But, it may be nothing—a shadow or a trick of the light. We don't see much detail."

"Yes, admiral," Kendrick said; "but we must prepare nonetheless."

"I'm well aware of that, captain," Talbot responded. "So, I brought this." He raises some papers. "These are old NASA procedures I rustled up. They address the discovery of an alien life specimen. Could you bloody-well believe it?" He passes them out.

"You've got to be shitting me," Cooper said.

"These procedures only account for alien life discovered on the Jupiter moons Ganymede and Europa," Kendrick said.

"Well, I have this, too," Talbot said.

He disseminates a copy of NASA's report of an alien specimen that was found on Mars on September 28, 2033 by the rover Excelsior. "It was found by a robot, and it never left the planet. This is all we have to go on."

"I can't help but see the irony," Malachy said.

"What do you mean?" Talbot asked.

"For centuries, man anticipated extraterrestrial life outside of our solar system. And now, after all this time, proof of life may have always been right under our noses."

Talbot smiles nervously. "We'll see."

"May I speak freely, sir?" Malachy asked Talbot.

Talbot nods.

"My hope is that the object turns out to be a meteor and nothing more. Perhaps it contains an unclassified, containable compound. My point is that any mere distraction has the potential of undermining the goals of our core mission..."

"Thank you, commander," Kendrick interrupted.

"Again, we don't entirely know what we have here," Talbot reassured.

"Perhaps we are obligated to find out," Malachy said.

"I'd sure like to know what this is," Cooper said.

Talbot picks up the documents and looks at them.

"According to NASA's procedures, we should not retrieve a living specimen," Talbot said. "If this is indeed the remains of an alien life form, it may very well be dead already and, under the circumstances, we may retrieve it only when it is deemed safe. Captain Wilcox says it's huge so, at best, we may only obtain a tissue sample—which may immediately degrade the moment it reaches the Moon's surface. If it's not deemed safe to disturb it, it may be best to record the find, document all of the details, and then isolate and contain it."

"I say we abandon Cabeus and go no further," Kendrick said. "Even Malachy agrees..."

"All I said was that the find serves as a distraction," Malachy interrupted. "Admiral, I'm in agreement with you."

"But, sir," Kendrick asserts; "there may be some form of contamination we could unleash."

"Lester, I want you to work with the base technicians," Talbot said. "I want a drill robot retrofitted to enable it to obtain samples for testing. Can you do that?"

"Yes, admiral," Malachy responded.

"Once we determine that whatever this mass contains is safe, then the base could remain in operation," Talbot said.

"I don't have a good feeling about this," Kendrick said.

"Captain, I would like a word with you in private, the two of you need to report to your stations and prepare for landing."

Malachy and Cooper quickly leave the conference room. Talbot stands over Kendrick.

"Sam, you are a fine officer with an impeccable record. That's why I selected you to serve as my executive officer." He leans into his face. "Never question me in front of other officers. If you disagree and there are others around, you bite hold of your tongue."

"Yes, admiral. But, I want to go on record by saying..."

"You're on record, captain. I'll see you on the bridge."

Talbot leaves.

\* \* \*

On Cabeus base, the drill team stand prepared at the top of the drill hole. The team leader, with both thumbs raised, commands the drilling apparatus.

"Lift! Lift!"

The apparatus begins to rise. It then begins to shake, and then, it sways almost violently.

"Abort! Abort!" The leader waves his arms.

The apparatus loses its footing and falls into the hole. Lights go out.

The team then sees movement deep in the shadowy hole. The shadows below grow larger until they reach the surface. Details come into focus until it becomes apparent that the base is in grave danger.

Several living, crawling creatures emerge at the knees of the stunned workers. For them, there is no escape.

# Chapter Six

Aboard the *Orpheus*, Fletcher steers the spacecraft ably during its final lunar orbit before descending. Talbot looks over newly-devised procedures when a communication reaches them.

"Admiral, we're receiving Cabeus," Anders said.

"Open communications," Talbot ordered.

*"Cabeus base to Orpheus, we're under attack."*

"Steve, what's going on?" Talbot responded.

*"Admiral, creatures surfaced from the hole—hundreds of them! They are tearing us apart, and there is no way to escape!"*

"Hold on, Steve! We're on the way!" Talbot turns to Fletcher. "How close are we?"

"Less than two hours away, sir," Fletcher answered.

*"Sir, we're out of time! The base walls are breaching!"*

Tearing sounds are heard over the *Orpheus* speaker.

*"Henry, tell my wife and son that I love them! Tell them—"*

Screams are followed by scurrying sounds. Then, static.

"Steve!" Talbot shouted. "...Steve?"

"We lost transmission, sir," Anders said.

"Fletcher, is there any way we can put this down quicker?" Talbot asked.

"No, sir," she answered.

Talbot slowly takes his chair and straps himself in. He lowers his head.

"Anders, inform the crew to prepare for landing," Talbot ordered.

"Yes, sir."

"C'mon, Steve," Talbot said at a whisper. "Hold on, buddy."

\* \* \*

The *Orpheus* kicks up a huge amount of dust while it descends onto the Moon's surface.

"Stand by for touch down," Fletcher said.

"Copy that," Kendrick responded.

"Ten meters... six meters... two meters... contact," Fletcher said.

"Engines stop!" Talbot ordered.

"The Orpheus has landed," Fletcher declared.

As crewmembers gaze out of the spacecraft's windows they view what remains of Cabeus base. Structures appear to have been torn open revealing cabin interiors, mechanical systems, wiring, and piping. Base lights still illuminate the grounds.

"My God!" Kendrick said.

"The power is still on," Talbot said. He turns to Kendrick. "There may be survivors. Let's suit up. I want you, Malachy, and two technicians." He turns to Anders. "Raise them."

"Yes, admiral."

While Talbot and Kendrick leave the bridge, Anders speaks into the microphone.

"Commander Malachy and technicians Taylor and Hudson, report to airlock," he said.

* * *

The men walk among the ruins surveying the damage. They hope to find survivors, but their hopes dwindle with each passing moment. What they do find, however, is evidence of an alien attack that initiated from a drill hole and radiated outward to all base facilities. Beyond a rocky ridge they find a strewn of human bodies and body parts. They see a lunar transport vehicle torn to pieces with dead astronauts inside. But, they see no creatures, alive or dead. Several sets of alien tracks, consisting of thick bristle and drag marks, lead away in various directions.

"They appear to have come from the same creature that we viewed in the photographs, except much smaller," Malachy said. "I'll estimate that they may be the size of a common canine."

"Offspring?" Kendrick asked Talbot.

"I suppose anything is possible now," Talbot answered.

As Talbot looks in the direction of some sets of tracks, a dreaded thought enters his mind.

"Wait, which direction is Tycho base?" he asked.

"We're already looking in that direction," Malachy said.

"Can we determine their speed?" Talbot asked. Kendrick answers abruptly.

"Sir, these are unknown creatures, and it's a lunar surface—it's almost impossible to estimate."

Talbot sees Malachy shaking his head in disgust inside his helmet.

"Well, captain," Malachy asserts; "when we consider the size of the prints and their relative distance apart while we also factor in the Moon's gravity..."

*"Orpheus to Admiral Talbot,"* blared Anders' voice inside their helmets.

"Talbot, here."

*"We received a communication from Tycho base. They are under attack, sir."*

"Shite! Ready the ship for immediate departure for Tycho," Talbot ordered. "And, notify the Peleus and the Cerberus. I need them to land at Eris 2 to evacuate that base."

\* \* \*

As Talbot and Kendrick enter the bridge, they hear Commander Meade's voice over the speaker.

*"Tycho base to Orpheus."*

"Commander, we are en route and one hour away," Talbot said in the microphone.

Over the speaker, the bridge hears strange, organic sounds. They have a steady tempo with a varying pitch; it sounds like language.

"Anders, record that," Talbot ordered.

*"Orpheus, I'm not alone."*

"Meade, what do you see?" Kendrick asked desperately.

*"Orpheus... we have a problem,"* Meade said in an eerily calm voice.

What the bridge hears next over the speaker are the sounds of destruction, screams.

"We need to find these creatures—all of them," Talbot declares in a voice for only Kendrick to hear; "they must be destroyed."

* * *

Eris 2 base concludes its evacuation procedures as the *Peleus* lands on its landing pad. Captain Mukai informs Commander Bower that the spacecraft is ready to receive evacuees.

While a *Peleus* crewmember assists base personnel on the Moon's surface, he sees a shadow move at the foot of a large boulder. He then sees another shadow move at the base of a rocky ridge. As he focuses his eyes, he sees them—crawling cautiously towards him. He speaks into his helmet microphone.

"Peleus, Clarke here. I see the creatures—lots of them—coming closer just southeast of the base, over."

*"Expedite evacuations!"* is trumpeted in his helmet. The crewmember grabs a few personnel while pushing others.

"Keep it moving, folks! Don't turn around—just keep it moving," he said while the creatures approach.

Just as the crewmember manages to push the remaining evacuee through the entry hatch, a creature grabs his leg. A tug of war match ensures as his spacesuit begins to rip. Air begins to suck out from a tear. In a desperate effort, the crewmember removes a wrench from a pocket and strikes the creature's head with it. The creature quickly releases its grip. The crewmember then springs into the hatch, which automatically closes behind him.

"Activate airlock," the crewmember said while catching his breath. While still holding the wrench, he notices a thick, dark gray liquid covering it. He then looks around at the evacuees. "Is everyone all right?"

As the *Peleus* lifts off, several creatures leap onto the spacecraft. This happens in full view of the bridge.

"Hard to port!" Captain Mukai ordered the pilot.

Many creatures fall back to the lunar surface while the spacecraft experiences a severe shimmy.

"Engine two has been compromised, captain!" the pilot declared.

"Hard to starboard! Full power!" Mukai ordered.

The remaining creatures fall back to the lunar surface. The captain sees an opportunity to escape.

"Ascend! Ascend!"

The *Peleus*, with a disabled engine, manages to lift off.

"Status report?" Mukai ordered.

"Engine one and three are burning. But, at best, we may only be able to maintain lunar orbit."

"Copy that," Mukai responded. "Initiate lunar orbiting sequence and notify the Orpheus of our status. I'll be in the medical galley with Clarke."

\* \* \*

"Peleus, once you obtain orbit, I want you to remain there until we rendezvous in one hour," Talbot ordered.

*"Understood, Orpheus,"*

"Anders, raise the Hyperion."

"Yes, admiral." He turns dials on his control panel and speaks into his microphone. "Orpheus to Hyperion."

*"Hyperion, here."*

"Mitchell, it's Talbot. I need you to evacuate all base personnel at Eris 1."

*"Roger that, admiral."*

"The Cerberus is about an hour behind you. I'll inform Briscoe to maneuver in support. Orpheus, out."

Talbot takes a deep breath and scratches his head.

"Anders, where are the Artemion and Gigantes?" he asked.

"They just departed from the Hephaestus."

"No, I want them to return to the Hephaestus and dock there."

Kendrick shifts in his chair.

\* \* \*

Commander Kadnikov affects final preparations for evacuating Eris 1 base. As he goes through his checklist, he hears a loud thud behind an interior wall.

"Sanchez, is that you?"

When no one answers, Kadnikov presses his head against the wall to listen. He then goes to his chair and speaks into a microphone.

"All base personnel, suit up now."

He then opens a huge cabinet that contains his spacesuit. He carefully suits up and locks his helmet in place. After tucking the digital base log under him armpit, he walks to his door and depresses the open button. The door slides open. Suddenly, standing upright before him is a substantial threat. Before he could react, his helmet containing his severed head crashes against the wall in the far corner of the room; his lifeless body then falls to the floor.

As Eris 1 is destroyed by the creatures, the *Hyperion* hovers above the landing pad. Several creatures perched on a nearby ridge leap onto the spacecraft and quickly begin to tear into the hull.

"Hull breach!" the pilot cried out.

"Contain it," Mitchell ordered.

"I can't, sir! The containment walls have been compromised. We are venting."

"Helmets on—everyone!"

"Captain, we're losing engines one and two! Our altitude is dropping fast!"

"Brace for impact!"

The *Hyperion* slams onto the Moon's surface and quickly explodes. All aboard perish.

The *Cerberus*, traveling above the crash, has just completed its final orbit before descending.

"Captain, your orders?" the pilot asked.

Before Briscoe could speak, she sees the creatures on the Moon's surface. Some of them unfurl what appears to be wings and take flight.

"Captain, they are heading right for us!" the pilot said.

"Evasive maneuvers!"

"They are approaching too rapidly!"

"We'll ram them," Briscoe ordered.

"Ma'am?"

"You heard me, pilot. Head straight for them, top speed."

"Range is sixty meters and closing... fifty... forty... thirty... twenty... ten. Brace for impact!"

The spacecraft slams into the creatures with such force that most of them fragment upon impact.

"Ascend, full power!" Briscoe ordered.

The *Cerberus* quickly climbs and enters lunar orbit.

"Deploy Devol now. I want any stragglers destroyed," she ordered.

While a preliminary damage report is compiled and while Talbot is notified of the fate of the Eris 1 base and the *Hyperion*, Devol enters airlock armed only with a pike and a large plastic disposal bag. After moving through the hatch, he sees no sign of alien life. What he does manage to find are some traces of the creatures and something even better.

"Devol to Captain Briscoe."

"Go ahead, Devol."

"No creatures survived, ma'am. I did find an entire specimen. It's intact but quite dead."

"Bag it and bring it on board."

"Yes, captain. Right away."

The creature, carefully wrapped, is quickly stored in a segregated refrigeration unit. The *Cerberus* then receives orders from Talbot to perform ship-to-ship docking with the *Peleus* to rescue its personnel and to leave that spacecraft in lunar orbit. Afterwards, the *Cerberus* will then dock with *Hephaestus* in Earth's orbit.

While the *Orpheus* tows the crippled *Peleus* to the *Hephaestus*, Malachy meets with Talbot.

"I have completed my analysis with Tesla of the recording of the creatures' sounds."

"What have you learned, Lester?"

"Admiral, based upon the sophisticated series of grunts and tweets, it does indeed resemble a form of language."

As the spacecraft leave lunar orbit, all Moon bases go dark.

\* \* \*

Aboard the *Hephaestus*, the creature lays on a brightly-lit table in the medical ward. Dr. Hailey Michels who is assigned to the space station as their senior scientist examined the creature. Bruno assisted her in the examination and is present for the presentation. Several officers are on hand, including Talbot, Kendrick, and Malachy. The presentation is recorded. Dr. Michels begins by introducing herself and all those in attendance.

"The specimen boasts a ferocious and efficient design. There is evidence of growth and maturation—this is an adult. Its exoskeleton is pressurized and is thick enough to withstand the rigors of outer space. Its broad head features multiple eyes—one central eye and two peripheral eyes on each side of the head; each set of eyes see different wavelengths: visible, ultraviolet, and infrared. Its mouth, here below central eye, has an extending proboscis with what appears to be four upper fangs and prehensile appendages around the mouth and under its thorax. It breathes in an unusual way. Whatever material that may exist is 'inhaled' between plates on its back. Its circulatory system consists of four hearts along the length of the body that slowly pump dark gray blood through thick, black vessels. Its blood is rich in metals such as iron and mercury.

Its legs are long, ten in total with five on each side, capable of navigating over most any terrain. Excretion occurs from the very rear. It body is so versatile that it has the capability to tuck its legs inside and roll into a ball similar to a pill bug."

"Armadillidium vulgare," Bruno said.

"What about its reproduction?" Talbot asked.

"It's parthenogenetic," Dr. Michels said. "However, it can only reproduce one like itself. Here are its eggs—some were already self-fertilized and growing. I viewed the photographs of the original large specimen and, although they are both the same species, they are quite different."

"This is a soldier," Bruno said. "It is an exceptional example of form-follows-function design."

"So, there are other types of creatures within this species?" Kendrick asked. "Not just male and female."

"It's quite possible," Dr. Michels answered. "Its metabolism is extremely slow. It converts ice into oxygen and stores it. It also ingests. We recovered the contents of its stomach: flesh from its parent—or queen."

"The queen prime, to be exact," Bruno said.

"Amazing," Malachy said.

"There is no way that this specimen could mate with the larger one," Dr. Michels continued; "so there may be others that serve as drones. It also has special retractable wings that may enable the creature to harness gravitational fields."

"It amazes me that there can be a creature that can survive the rigors of outer space," Kendrick said.

"Hypsibius dujardini," Bruno retorted.

"What?"

"A tardigrade has been proven to survive in outer space, captain," Bruno clarified.

"What is its life expectancy?" Malachy asked.

"This specimen is extremely old," Dr. Michels answered.

"How old?"

"Between periods of hibernation? Centuries," Bruno answered.

They all look at one another.

"So, what do we call them?" Talbot asked. "Do we have a name?"

"Bruno came up with something," Dr. Michels said. "Bruno?"

"Lunadites."

* * *

While most *Orpheus* crewmembers are asleep in their quarters, Malachy emerges and enters the *Hephaestus*. He travels down a corridor to the medical ward. He finds the refrigeration chamber where the creature is stored. He opens the drawer.

"Hello, my friend," he whispered.

While he strokes its spiny legs, his finger pricks something sharp. Blood flows from the small wound. He quickly wraps it in gauze that he finds in a small, white cabinet. He then takes a last look at the creature before leaving.

* * *

To destroy the lunadites, the *Hephaestus* technicians with the assistance of Cooper arm the

*Orpheus* and *Cerberus* with industrial laser cannons derived from drilling technology.

"We can't burn them in space, but we can sure hell disrupt them," Cooper said.

After the *Peleus* engine is repaired, it is also fortified with these weapons.

Several crewmembers are issued hastily fashioned electro-plasma rifles, again from drilling technology, and are fitted with special jetpacks to battle the lunadites in space. Drilling robots intended to operate on Cabeus base are retrofitted for battle in space. All three spacecraft, the *Orpheus*, *Cerberus*, and *Peleus*, depart in triangular attack formation for the Moon.

* * *

The tide turns in favor of the humans. Many of the lunadites are destroyed at the Moon by the spacecraft weapons, jetpack-clad crewmembers, and laser-firing robots. However, swarms of lunadites manage to escape from the Moon's surface and get past the spacecraft toward Earth. They deploy wings to harness the gravitational field between the Moon and the Earth. The spacecraft quickly pursue them.

* * *

Malachy's injury heals, but the skin on his hand slightly darkens. He also feels different. He keeps this to himself.

# Chapter Seven

"Lunadites approaching, captain!" the *Hephaestus* pilot shouted.

Carmichael hastily speaks into the microphone.

"All crewmembers, suit up forthwith and report to airlock for deployment. Attack is imminent! Repeat, attack is imminent!"

He turns to the communications officer.

"Raise the Orpheus."

"They're already raising us, sir," the communications officer responded.

"Admiral, are you missing some of these little bastards?" Carmichael asked.

*"Ian, we're in pursuit right now,"* Talbot said. *"Hold them off the best you can. Don't allow any one of them—not one of them—to get past you and descend on Earth!"*

"Roger that, admiral. We'll do our best."

Carmichael sits in his chair and looks down at his digital console. He mentally calculates when the lunadites will arrive. He thinks 20 minutes. He turns to the robot.

"Bruno, how long do we have?"

"Twenty-one minutes, forty-four point five seconds."

* * *

The *Orpheus* is maintaining top speed while ramming several lunadites. Those at farther distances are destroyed by laser cannons. Anders serves as the gunner.

"So many of them," Talbot said. "How much longer, Fletcher?"

"Twenty-seven minutes, fifteen seconds."

"Can't we push this rusted can?" Talbot said with exacerbation.

"Hey, Coop, why don't you get out and push?" Kendrick said.

"There is no time for joking, captain—people are dying," Talbot said sternly.

"I am well aware of that, admiral. I don't need to be reminded."

"How far behind are the Cerberus and the Peleus?" Talbot asked.

"Minutes, sir," Fletcher asked.

"C'mon, Ian," Talbot says to himself. "Hang in there."

* * *

"Captain, the lunadites are in sight," the *Hephaestus* pilot said.

"Dispatch crewmembers," Carmichael ordered. "And I want those robots out there in support."

"Yes, sir," the communications officer said.

Jetpack crewmembers with electro-plasma rifles and laser-firing robots leave the airlock hatch and drift into space. They assemble into attack formation. Upon command, they send out the first volley of blasts. A few of the lunadites manage to penetrate the attack and advance on to the *Hephaestus.*

"With the captain's permission, I wish to join the fight," Bruno asked.

"Go get 'em!" Carmichael responded.

Bruno hastily reports to the airlock. He grabs a rifle and exits through the hatch. He fires striking many of them with perfect precision. He continues firing until the weapon malfunctions. He then swings the weapon and strikes one with such force that it instantly kills it. A few more approach it as he continues to swing, successfully striking more. Other lunadites avoid the space station altogether and advance onto Earth. Bruno assesses the damage and no longer sees immediate danger. He sees the *Orpheus* approaching. He also sees the *Cerberus* and the *Peleus* at a greater distance. The robot reenters the space station.

Many lunadites then enter Earth's atmosphere as the *Orpheus* arrives. Crewmembers witness the creatures' wings retract. It is night at the face of the Earth where the lunadites navigate. They fix on the brightest target of the coastal Atlantic Ocean.

"It looks like they're targeting New York City," Talbot said.

The lunadites tightly roll into balls. They then resemble a storm for fiery meteors as they enter Earth's stratosphere. After a short time, they splash land approximately twenty kilometers from New York harbor. The oxygen-rich Earth enables the metabolism of these creatures to quicken. They swiftly emerge onto the Brooklyn shore and assemble into attack formation. During their march on the city streets, they attack several people and disable a number of autocars. The local police respond, draw their pistols, and fire upon them. More officers respond; more lunadites are killed.

The humans are victorious by the time the state national guards arrive.

# Chapter Eight

After Talbot receives word of the victory on Earth, he orders immediate repairs to the *Hephaestus* and directs the *Cerberus* to report to the Moon while the *Orpheus* and *Peleus* remain with the space station.

As the *Cerberus* engages trans-lunar injection, it does not encounter any remaining lunadites. Captain Briscoe keeps constant contact with Talbot. She speaks with him on a private communication panel in his quarters.

*"Lunar synchronous orbit in two hours, admiral,"* Briscoe said.

"Ellie, be careful. We need to secure the Moon and reengage our original mission. The Moon's trajectory must be corrected and that crucial window in time is closing fast."

*"Roger that."*

"After all this is done, you do realize that we have some unfinished business."

*"And, what might that be?"*

"A tropical landscape, a secluded beach..."

*"Fresh fruit? God, I miss fresh fruit."*

"Just give us the go-ahead and get yourself back to me. We have a world to save," Talbot said with a broad smile."

*"Copy that, my love."*

\* \* \*

At Cabeus base, deep within the drill hole, there is movement. The ground breaks as a behemoth slowly rises to the surface. It is another queen prime that was hibernating even deeper in the ice. After its entire mass is freed from the gray rock, it arches its back. From in between the several crevices of its armor plates it deploys thousands of offspring consisting of battle-ready soldiers. Drones and queens also emerge and take flight. After one orbit around the Moon, their heading is Earth.

*"Cerberus to Orpheus, come in?"*

"Orpheus here," Anders said.

*"We see them—a multitude of them, and they're heading right for us,"* the communications officer exclaimed.

"Order the admiral to the bridge!" Kendrick shouted to Anders. "Captain Briscoe, are you there?"

*"Here, captain. The number is more than we ever faced."*

"Get out of there; there's nothing you can do," Kendrick ordered.

*"We're trying, but they're pursuing us and closing,"* she responded. In the background of Captain Briscoe's transmission, Kendrick hears, *"...thirty meters... twenty-five..."*

Talbot enters the bridge and immediately takes his chair.

"Briscoe, report!" he transmitted with desperation.

*"Admiral, we have a hull breach on deck two! We will attempt to contain it, but we are also losing gravity control... Henry?*

"I'm here, Ellie!"

*I'll have to give you a rain check for that tropical setting we talked about..."*

"Ellie?... Ellie?!"

The transmission ends in static.

\* \* \*

The first band of lunadites that consist of one queen, several drones and hundreds of soldiers, enter Earth's atmosphere. They splash land in the Pacific Ocean on the South American coast. As they emerge onto Lima, Peru, they immediately establish a nest. The drones surround the queen as she sheds hundreds of offspring. Hieratical structures are quickly established and fortified while hordes of lunadites disperse to occupy and control the entire continent.

While the lunadite soldiers move over land they also shed offspring. The young soldiers quickly fall into rank and file formations and prepare to feed by stroking their proboscises. As they march, they destroy everything in their wake; very little stands in their way.

A myriad of lunadites occupy South Africa and rapidly move north. They feed and multiply as they march. The skies are so thick with them that darkness overtakes the midday sky. The next band of lunadites, consisting of a few thousand, makes their landing in southern Mongolia. The queen quickly assumes control and sends her minions throughout Asian and into Europe.

In Chicago, hundreds of drone lunadites smash through the tall windows of the main ASERA building and crawl from floor to floor tearing the panicked people to shreds. From his penthouse office, Marcus Terrell watches a shower of lunadites rain down on the entire city. On his desk are unencrypted secret reports addressed to him from Malachy conveying intelligence information on Talbot's conduct and decision making during his entire command. Huge shards of glass fall from above as the creatures enter the room. They quickly approach Terrell as he covers his face. His screams are silenced when his chest is split open. His blood splatters on the ornate walls.

While in Earth's orbit, the *Peleus* continues to pursue and fire upon the lunadites. It is not long before they converge upon the spacecraft, take hold of it, and breach its hull.

\* \* \*

While the *Orpheus* entered the Moon's orbit, it received the final transmission of the *Peleus*. However, the *Orpheus* continues on its course to the Cabeus base to destroy the second queen prime. It was only a matter of minutes before the target was in range.

"Target acquired, admiral," Anders said.

"Fire."

The cannon fire raddles the spacecraft. The explosion on the surface consists of a large, billowing gray accumulation of dust. Cabeus base is completely destroyed.

"Okay, let's get back to the Hephaestus," Talbot ordered.

Just as the spacecraft makes preparations to leave lunar orbit, Fletcher and Anders detect objects that register on a collision course. When Fletcher changed course slightly, the objects also changed course.

"Joan, this is fucked up!" Anders said.

"I know it, Ken," she said. She turns to Talbot. "Lunadites ahead, admiral."

"Anders, fix your target," he orders.

"I have them spotted, sir. They'll be in range in under a minute."

"Should we ram them?" Fletcher asked.

"No, evasive maneuvers!"

"Aye, sir!"

As the *Orpheus* avoids a swarm, a few soldiers manage to grab hold of the spacecraft. One tears the hull open and enters inside.

"Hull breach, admiral. Deck three," Fletcher said aloud.

"Containment!" Talbot orders.

His ASERA mug slowly floats.

"We're losing gravity control!" he shouted. "Compensate!" he ordered Anders.

"Compensating now, sir."

The mug then falls to the floor and breaks.

"Gravity back, sir."

"Fuck, that was my favorite mug!" Talbot grabs an electro-plasma rifle and switches it on. It lights up and hums.

"I'm going to deck three," he said as he left the bridge.

As Talbot reaches the bottom of forward ladder two, he is met by Tesla.

"Why are you not attacking the invader?" he asked the robot. "It's here on this deck!"

Tesla grabs Talbot's rifle and attempts to take it from him. Talbot pulls back.

"What are you doing you fucking robot? I order you to..."

Tesla dislodges the rifle from Talbot's hands and throws him to the floor. It then levels the rifle at him and fires. The blast rips into Talbot's abdomen. Tesla then turns and runs toward the aft section of the ship while leaving Talbot mortally wounded.

As Tesla moves through a narrow corridor, it then turns and faces a lunadite. The creature lifts its huge, spiny-sharp tibias.

"It would have been fascinating to analyze you," Tesla said in a regretful tone.

The robot is quickly decapitated. However, it remains standing while still holding the rifle. It lowers the muzzle and fires killing the creature. Tesla then drops the rifle and retrieves its head on the floor behind it. It carefully carries the object to the robot shop.

On the bridge, Fletcher declares an emergency. When Talbot doesn't respond, he grabs a rifle, leaves the bridge, and makes his way to deck three. On the floor, he finds Talbot. He kneels beside him and attempts to assess the injury.

"No, don't," Talbot said almost at a whisper.

"Admiral?"

"Order an immediate abandonment of the spacecraft. The crew stands a better chance in the ALMs."

"Yes, sir."

Talbot removes the key from around his neck.

"Here," he said while he gives him the key. "You must insert this into the Hephaestus computer. It will initiate the Exodus Program."

"What is that?"

Talbot takes a deep breath.

"The Exodus Program was created when it was learned in 2109 that a deadly asteroid may be en route toward Earth. The program serves as a means of escape from Earth's inhalation. I think we both know that our current circumstance warrants action."

"What do I do?"

"Just insert the key. It will all be explained to you. It was a pleasure serving with..."

"Admiral?"

Talbot dies.

\* \* \*

Two lunadites enter the *Orpheus* on deck three. They swiftly move in different directions.

Malachy, while making his way to his quarters, finds himself facing a lunadite. The creature is about to strike when it stops. It looks deeply into Malachy's eyes and turns away. Malachy then resumes his scamper to his quarters.

Over the ship's speakers, the order is given by Kendrick to abandon the spacecraft. Crewmembers immediately report to the ALMs. Within minutes, both aft ALMs deploy. After another minute, a forward ALM deploys.

When Malachy arrives at his quarters, he quickly grabs Tesla's head and guides its body aboard a nearby forward lifeboat. Other crewmembers enter the vessel, including Fletcher and Anders, and all take seats. Kendrick then enters.

"This is it, Fletcher. Get us out of here," Kendrick ordered.

Fletcher depresses the hatch lever and the ALM is sealed. With a substantial jolt, the vessel is underway. From small windows, the crewmembers watch the *Orpheus* as it gets torn apart by the lunadites.

Kendrick looks across at Malachy. While he studies him, he feels his suspicion get the better of him. Malachy ignores Kendrick and, instead, turns his attention to Tesla as he begins to repair it.

\* \* \*

The takeover of the Earth by the lunadites is underway. Mass extinction is imminent, but there are some regions that remain unaffected.

While aboard the ALM, Kendrick receives a message from the *Hephaestus* that the command headquarters has been obliterated.

"You are the supreme commander now, captain," Malachy told Kendrick with a grin. Kendrick ignores him. He turns to Fetcher.

"How far along are we?"

"The Hephaestus will be visible within five minutes," she answered.

"Raise Cooper in ALM-F1," Kendrick ordered Fletcher. She does so.

*"Cooper, here."*

"Coop, I need to speak with you as soon as I arrive. Where are you?"

*"We're about to dock, sir. ALM-A1 and A2 are already docking. Also, the Artemion and Gigantes have already docked."*

"Okay, I'll see you in a few minutes. Oh, and one more thing: Talbot is dead. Kendrick, out."

* * *

After the ALM docks with the *Hephaestus* with the remaining survivors of the *Orpheus*, Kendrick grabs Cooper.

"How many survivors, Coop?"

"Carmichael tells me almost one-hundred." He points. "There he is now."

"Ian, over here!" Kendrick called out. Carmichael walks over.

"Captain, I'm glad to see that you're all right," he said. "Talbot?"

"No," he said slowly while shaking his head. "I need you to take me to the ship's computer, now," he ordered.

"Right away, sir."

The three men race to the computer. When they arrive, Kendrick tells Carmichael to open the mainframe panel. Carmichael does so. Kendrick looks closely for the key slot.

"Here it is," Kendrick declared.

"What is it," Carmichael asked.

Kendrick inserts the key.

"It's a chance at survival," he said while turning the key.

The computer screen displays images, charts, and plans. Exodus spacecraft and launch stations are displayed. Some data is encrypted, but that plans are quite clear.

"Let me get Bruno in here," Carmichael said. "It can help us initiate this plan."

Carmichael speaks into a microphone.

"In the meantime," Kendrick continues; "we must ready both transport ships and all ALMs for departure to the Exodus launch stations. It looks like there are a few of them. So, we need to determine who goes where. We cannot delay departures."

Bruno enters the computer room.

"Did you send for me, sir?" it asked.

"Bruno, talk to the computer. Extract everything relating to the Exodus Program."

"Yes, sir. Spacecraft is designated exodus class, intergalactic, and there are six in total. The size of each spacecraft is three-hundred eleven point seven meters long, two-hundred eight point twenty-one meters wide, and one-hundred four point eighty-five meters high. Each has an acceleration of ninety-eight thousand, one-hundred twenty kilometers per hour with an endurance of forty years. The escape system for each spacecraft consists of eight ALMs. All exodus spacecraft were manufactured by Lockheed Martin under the top-secret specifications of Dr. Calvin Westbrook."

"These ships are rather sizable," Cooper said. "What sort of propulsion system are we talking about?"

"Exodus Program spacecraft propulsion consists of three stage," Bruno continues. "The first is a delivery system stage via chemical combustion engines that deliver the spacecraft out of Earth's orbit. These engines are then jettisoned. The second is an operational system stage via ion propulsion thrusters that allow the spacecraft to navigate outside of the Earth's solar system and onward in interstellar space—the thrusters use electronically-charged xenon gas as a propellant. The third and final stage is the trans-interstellar stage via ramjet fusion engines that use hydrogen in space as a propulsion source—each engine has a scoop in front that collects hydrogen, fuses it, and shoots out a stream of hydrogen. Solar panels, like wings, expose to access light in order to generate power."

"Perpetual energy?" Kendrick asked.

"Yes, sir. The spacecraft boasts eight-thousand, nine-hundred solar cells and one-thousand, two-hundred cylindrical lenses that focus the light on the cells. Cruising speed is six-hundred seventy five point ninety-two kilometers per second, or two-million, four-hundred thirty-three thousand, three-hundred twenty-eight point thirteen kilometers per hour. Conceived and designed in top-secrecy by Dr. Westbrook. The manufacturer was Northrop Grumman Systems. All spacecraft navigation is operated with a pre-programed destination."

"What is the destination?" Kendrick asked.

"Accessing... Planet 91C," Bruno answered. "It is a planet determined most suitable for human life discovered during the Kepler-4 mission in 2084. The planet is five percent larger than Earth and maintains a three-hundred eighty-four day orbit in the habitable zone of a sun-like star in the constellation Cygnus. Its distance is one-thousand, eight-hundred seventeen light years from Earth."

Cooper whistles. "That's pretty far."

"How do we survive?" Kendrick asked.

"Here are the plans, captain," Bruno said. A series of illustrations and photographs display on the screen. "Suspended animation. Bodies are put in chemically-induced hibernation via inhalation of hydrogen sulfide and are placed within sealed cryogenic chambers, pictured here."

"The body can sustain this?" Cooper asked.

"Theoretically, yes," Bruno answered; "especially if it is done right."

"Explain, Bruno," Kendrick said.

"While the body is carefully preserved in the chamber, the life process is significantly slowed down. Heart rate is reduced to ten beats per minute, respiration decreased to four breaths per minute, and core body temperature is dropped to six degrees Celsius. Metabolism is maintained via oxygen conservation and carbon dioxide production is decreased by a factor of twenty. Similar systems exist for dogs."

"Dogs?"

"Yes, dogs," Bruno answers. "Man's best friend—next to robots, of course."

"Theoretically?" Cooper said. "Well, I'm in!"

"Gee, Coop, there doesn't seem to be much of a choice," Kendrick said with a smile. He turns to Carmichael. "I will immediately notify the Exodus bases. What are they, Bruno?"

"Touros, Brazil, Cape Canaveral, Florida, and Baikonur Cosmodrome, Kazakh Steppe, Russia."

"Very well. We initiate launches from Earth in four hours."

\* \* \*

Malachy secretly obtains information from the *Hephaestus*'s computer. He learns of the Exodus Program. As he attempts to initiate shutdown sequence to compromise the spacecraft's computer system, Kendrick and Cooper enter the computer room.

"What are you doing?" Kendrick said. "Stop!"

Malachy lunges for Kendrick. Cooper attempts to stop this attack with a wrench. Malachy strikes him and quickly delivers him to the floor. Kendrick then engages Malachy by punching him in the face. He then kicks Malachy in the head sending him back into a wall. Malachy emerges. The skin on his face is gashed and bleeding a thick, dark gray liquid.

"What the fuck?" Cooper exclaimed.

Malachy tears off part of his face revealing black, hard-scaled skin underneath. He then rips the skin off his hand exposing a hideously-sharp extremity. As he is about to retaliate, Fletcher arrives with an electro-plasma rifle and shoots Malachy in the shoulder. Wounded, he hastily retreats to find an escape.

Bruno appears.

"May I be of assistance?" it asked. Kendrick turns to him.

"Bruno, kill that *creature*."

"Yes, captain."

Bruno takes chase, but Malachy manages to obtain Tesla and escape aboard a *Hephaestus* ALM. Bruno gazes out of the window to see the vessel embark toward Earth.

* * *

Captain James "Jim" Ashby, the commander of the Touros, Brazil, launch base directs evacuations and the launch procedures of *Exodus* 1-A and *Exodus* 1-B. After both spacecraft make their way from the vehicle assembly hanger, they sit on Launch Complexes 2 and 3, respectively, fueling for the long flight ahead. Aboard the spacecraft, among other items on their vast manifests, are a variety of seeds for edible plantation, hydroponic systems, and dogs, as ordered. The launches of both spacecraft are successfully expedited in two hours.

On the *Hephaestus*, Kendrick sets the space station on a gradual collision course with Earth by degrading the ship's orbit. Half of the evacuees, including Bruno, board the *Artemion* and plot a course for Cape Canaveral, Florida. Before Kendrick boards this transport, he supervises the boarding of the *Gigantes*. Its destination is Kazakh Steppe, Russia. The *Artemion* and the *Gigantes* are underway within an hour.

Captain Scott Cochran, the commander of the launch base at Cape Canaveral, Florida, carefully moves *Exodus* 2-A, *Exodus* 2-B, and *Exodus* 2-C from the vehicle assembly building onto Launch Complexes 39C, 39B, and 39A, respectively—the same launch pads used in the manned Mars missions. From where he commands, Cochran can see the lunadites flying about. He installs his second-in-command as commander of *Exodus* 2-B and orders its immediate launch. It clears its tower.

One hour later, the *Artemion* lands at Cape Canaveral. Kendrick quickly meets with Cochran to expedite launches.

"Captain, attacks are imminent," Cochran expressed.

"Okay, wheels up!"

Kendrick takes command of *Exodus* 2-A while Cochran takes *Exodus* 2-C. Launch is expedited in one hour and just in time. The lunadites trample on the launch grounds as both spacecraft clear their towers. However, as *Exodus* 2-C pitches, it malfunctions and explodes. All aboard perish.

At the Baikonur Cosmodrome, Kazakh Steppe, Russia, launch base, Captain Dimitry Kraimir assumes command of *Exodus* 3. While it sits fully-fueled on Pad 39 at Site 200, the *Gigantes* arrives with its complement and safely lands. The launch is expedited in under two hours.

# Epilogue

Exodus spacecraft speed away on a heading for Planet 91C. Its crewmembers are not entirely certain whether the lunadites will survive the loss of the Moon. But, by this time, it doesn't matter to any of them. All they have are memories and each other.

The highly-advanced on-craft robotic systems, or Exodus caretaker robots, prepare crewmembers in bands for their long hibernation. Bruno proves to be very helpful in this endeavor.

Aboard *Exodus* 2-A, Fletcher meets with Kendrick.

"Captain, do you have a minute?"

"Sure, Joan."

"I just wanted to say that I'm very proud at the way you've taken command. We're all alive because of you."

"Well... I want to thank you for the way you handle a rifle." Kendrick smiles.

"Captain, I—"

"Joan, call me Sam."

"Sam, I'm so scared about our future. Everything is so uncertain."

"Hey, the important thing is that we're together, and that we're safe for now."

Before Kendrick utters another word, Fletcher plants a passionate kiss on his lips. Just then, Cooper walks into the room.

"Hey, Sammy!—oops! I'm sorry! I'll come back later."

"You do that, Coop," Fletcher said with a broad smile while still looking at Kendrick.

Cooper smiles and leaves the room. Kendrick and Fletcher embrace and resume their kiss.

As *Exodus* 2-A gracefully moves in interstellar space, something is seen clinging to a partially hidden panel. A sole lunadite latches tight. One of its appendages twitches as the thrusters ignite.

30538848R00069

Made in the USA
Charleston, SC
18 June 2014